CW00494716

NO MAN IS AN ISLAND

NO MAN IS AN ISLAND

JOSEPH HUCKNALL

The Book Guild Ltd

First published in Great Britain in 2021 by
The Book Guild Ltd
9 Priory Business Park
Wistow Road, Kibworth
Leicestershire, LE8 0RX
Freephone: 0800 999 2982
www.bookguild.co.uk
Email: info@bookguild.co.uk
Twitter: @bookguild

Copyright © 2021 Joseph Hucknall

The right of Joseph Hucknall to be identified as the author of this work has been asserted by him in accordance with the Copyright, Design and Patents Act 1988.

All rights reserved. No part of this publication may be reproduced, transmitted, or stored in a retrieval system, in any form or by any means, without permission in writing from the publisher, nor be otherwise circulated in any form of binding or cover other than that in which it is published and without a similar condition being imposed on the subsequent purchaser.

This work is entirely fictitious and bears no resemblance to any persons living or dead.

Typeset in Adobe Garmond Pro

Printed and bound by CPI Group (UK) Ltd, Croydon, CR0 4YY

ISBN 978 1913551 742

Cover image: Detail from William Hogarth's 'A Harlot's Progress'.
Metropolitan Museum of Art, Harris Brisbane Dick Fund, 1932.

British Library Cataloguing in Publication Data.
A catalogue record for this book is available from the British Library.

MIX
Paper from responsible sources
FSC® C013604

To Ramōn Gonzalez – Partner & Soulmate.

Author of *The Boy In A Turban* & *A life's Tales*

1

LONDON 1751

'His Highness is asking for you, James,' said Prince Frederick's manservant, putting his head round the door.

James turned to his music pupil, Augusta, who was named after her mother but familiarly known as Gusta.

'Continue your practise while I'm with your father. There is no need for you to stop playing,' James told her, and, turning to her younger siblings, George and Elizabeth, said, 'And you just listen quietly to Gusta. You can both play when I return.'

Gusta emitted a long, audible sigh of impatience. 'Father is always interrupting our lessons.'

'That's because he's very interested in the progress you're making at your piano lessons. Would you wish it to be otherwise?' asked James as he hurriedly left the room before Gusta could reply.

Gusta screwed up her nose to show that she was not convinced by her tutor's reasoning. She was fourteen and the eldest child of Prince Frederick, and of an age to question adults' motives. Growing up in her father's court, she was used to being given many excuses by overprotective servants which she later invariably found out to be untrue, so she rarely believed any of them now. She bore her seniority to her siblings seriously, and with her high forehead, oval face, long nose and bulging eyes, she had an unmistaken resemblance to her father.

As James walked through the corridors of Leicester House, he thought that the reason for the interruption of the lessons would very likely be otherwise. More likely, it would be for him to give a piano concert at the Court or to accompany the prince and his sisters at their music or even more likely about the cricket game arranged to be played at the weekend.

Being a mulatto, James's presence stood out whenever he was in the company of white people. His skin was a dark tawny colour and his features were more African from his mother than of his white father. His curly black hair confirmed his Negroid origins when it was not covered by a fashionable wig. His amiable manner showed in his face by a ready smile and eyes which opened wide when his interest was aroused.

He hesitated before knocking on the door of the prince's drawing room and waited.

'Come in!'

As he entered, he quickly took in the scene. Prince Frederick was seated at the table with several books and a map spread out in front of him. He was dressed in a red silk coat trimmed with gold brocade, his hair drawn back and tied with a red ribbon. The prince looked towards James, then relaxed back into the chair when he saw who had entered and smiled engagingly at him.

'Ah, James! Good to see you. How are my children progressing today? Well, I hope? But they are not what I wish to talk to you about now, but you, James, yourself. You are in a unique position in my court, you know, for not only are you my children's music master, which distinguishes you, but you are the only person in my court of the African race. Such an interesting continent, Africa, and with so much of our country's wealth coming out of its African trade.'

The prince paused as he looked at James, sizing him up, as if seeing him for the first time.

'But I do confess that I am so very ignorant of the African mind that I hope you can throw some light onto it for me,' he continued with a smile. 'Indeed, I am not sure if I know the English mind, not having grown up with it. But it is the future I am looking to, when I eventually succeed to the throne. Papa only looks to Europe and the wars with France.'

The prince sighed at the thought before smiling sardonically and raising an eyebrow. 'Hopefully he will not have long to live and then I can rule in peace.'

'Yes, Your Highness, but I have no experience of Africa and can barely remember my own childhood in Jamaica without misery,' said James, anxious to avoid acknowledgement of the prince's opposition to the king.

'That may be so, but your very colour distinguishes itself in my court and, I hear, causes anguish to Papa and Mama, much to my delight. So, you see, James, your presence here is greatly appreciated by me. And I know how well my children think of you. You show such tact and patience with them. You have a surprising understanding of children, James.'

'Thank you, Your Highness. It's my honour to hold such a position.'

'Ah, so, James! You are fortunate indeed not to have parents denying your inheritance and shouting abuse at you as mine do. Now, how is your cricket? You are playing at the weekend, aren't you?'

'Yes, Your Highness. I'm looking forward to it very much,' replied James, relieved at the turn of the conversation.

The prince leant further back in his chair and stretched out his long legs. He was tall and ungainly with an oval face and a prominent nose set between large, rather bulging eyes.

'And so am I! Oh, to feel the ball in my hand and to bowl someone out,' exclaimed the prince. 'But the batting, James, the batting! That is something else. I must foster the game so that more Englishmen learn to enjoy it. I insist that all my children come to watch and get an understanding of the game, and my wife, Augusta, too, although I know she's not so keen on it. Pity it was not played in Hanover. Will your wife be coming too?'

'Yes, I understand so, Your Highness, and her mother.'

'Ah, splendid, and do bring them to my soirée in the evening. My sisters and I will be playing our cellos,' said the prince.

'Thank you, Your Highness, I'm sure they will be delighted to come,' James responded.

The prince put on a sombre look and gave another long sigh. 'I was very sorry to hear of Mr Kent's death. Such a tragic loss to architecture. Lord Burlington was greatly bereaved at the death of so good a friend. A pity that Kent didn't marry, but then that is why men take mistresses, although the king does both and boasts about it. Such a mockery of marriage, and to any other wife but Mama it would be an insult, but then I would expect nothing less of my parents. I believe in fidelity once you are married.'

It appeared that the prince needed to declare his hatred of his parents to anyone in his presence, but James felt uncomfortable listening to the diatribe. He knew that his position in Court did not warrant the sharing of such confidences. There were many in the prince's court who would have heaped coals onto the fire of the prince's continual war with his parents, many of whom looked forward to his succession to improve their own position, but James saw them as disruptive to any healing of the rift between the king and his parents and, out of respect, kept his silence.

As he returned to the music room, he reflected on his transition from his Caribbean origins to his musical achievements and his position at the court. Not a day passed when he did not think of his good fortune and question himself whether he was worthy of it. As to having an "African mind", as the prince had said, he was not aware of having anything other than an English mind, if there was such a thing, but was he fooling himself of that, as well? How could he, born of a black mother, a slave, claim to have an English mind any more than he could claim to have white skin?

Arriving back at the music room, he stood outside the door to hear whether the children were continuing their practise and was not surprised to overhear them talking instead.

'I tell you it *is* sunburn,' Gusta said emphatically.

'I told you to continue your practise,' said James on opening the door.

Gusta looked at him defiantly. 'George was asking me why you were a different colour to us and I told him it was because of the sun. Everyone knows that Africa is hot and the sun burns you.'

'Well, you are right in a way, but my colour is not caused by the sun. Some think it is for our natural protection of the skin from the sun. Darker skin reduces the impact of sunlight. If I was white and lived in Africa, then it would burn me.'

'But you have told us that you did not come from Africa,' said Gusta.

'No, but my mother did.'

'And was she black?'

'Yes.'

'And your father? Did he come from Africa, too?'

'Er, no. He was white.'

James thought back to the plantation and to the massa who had sold him to the captain sixteen years ago. His mother had once told him that the massa was his father, but he had questioned it ever since, as he never remembered him behaving like a father. What father would sell his own son?

James could see Gusta trying to unravel the mystery of his origins and spoke before she could ask any more questions. 'I think you should concentrate on your music now,' he said to Gusta. 'Play your ballet pieces from Monsieur Lully, and George and Elizabeth can dance to them.'

'I don't want to dance,' said George, who was twelve years old and, although shy, was already known for his stubbornness. 'I would rather you tell us about your voyage to England when you were little and being kidnapped. Tell us again how you escaped.'

'No, I have told you already, and this is your music lesson. Your father will want to know how you are all progressing, and I want to give him a good report, so let us now concentrate on your playing.'

George was not to be put off and looked at James intently. 'Grandpa told me that you must have been a slave once.'

'Grandpa knows everything. He's the king,' said Gusta firmly.

'He told me that I will be king after Papa and that I will make a good king,' said George.

'Well, I won't curtsy to you,' said Gusta, putting on a disapproving look.

'I will. I'll curtsy to you like this,' said the ten-year-old Elizabeth, and demonstrated such an exaggerated curtsy that she nearly fell over, causing them all to laugh.

'Were you really once a slave, James?' asked George in a serious tone.

'I suppose I was born one, but I never thought of myself as one. Although the captain bought me at a slave auction, he brought me up as his own son. Now let us resume our music.'

'He bought you?' questioned Gusta in her usual disbelieving manner. 'For how much?'

'Yes. He paid ten pounds.'

Gusta was silent for a while as she considered the implications. 'Ten pounds? That is a lot of money. Did they weigh you?'

James laughed at the question, but then his mind went back to the auction and he remembered being the last slave standing, being poked, prodded and appraised, fearful of the unknown and hoping that no one would bid for him so that he could go back to his mother and the plantation. He remembered Captain Cudlip bidding for him and then buying him his first pair of shoes, and the weight he felt when he put them on. The thought brought him back to Gusta's unanswered question.

‘Weigh me?’ he asked absentmindedly. His reverie had been so realistic that momentarily he had been lost in the past.

Gusta was standing in front of him, waiting. ‘Yes, did they weigh you?’ she repeated impatiently.

‘No, they just sized each one of us up and made a bid for the fittest-looking, but that was a long time ago. Now let us get back to the present and resume our music lesson.’

George was getting fidgety and confronted James. ‘No. I’ve had enough music today,’ he said assertively. ‘Are you playing cricket at Clivedon on Saturday? Papa said I can play on his side.’

‘Yes, I’m playing. Let us hope the weather allows us to. It’s only spring and very early to start playing,’ said James. ‘Now, please let us continue with the lesson.’

George stood his ground, as was his habit, rarely giving in to persuasion. ‘Well, it’s sunny now, and I’m going to the garden to get some cricket practice in,’ he said, getting ready to leave the room.

Gusta stood in front of him and assumed a look of authority. ‘You are not to go until James says so. Anyway, you can’t play cricket on your own, so with James’s permission, I’ll go with you.’

James realised that today’s lesson had come to its natural conclusion and picked up the music sheets with a sigh. ‘Yes, I think we may as well finish the lesson for today, but next time, I ask for no interruption.’

Gusta hung back as her brothers lost no time and ran out of the room. ‘If you were once a slave, how did you learn music?’ she asked abruptly.

‘It was on the ship that brought me here, the *Annabelle*. One of the crew, Patch, it was. He played the fiddle and taught me. He said that I had an ear for music and the crew encouraged me to play for them.’

James thoughts went back to the ship that brought him to England, the *Annabelle*, to Captain Cudlip and his motley crew, and to Patch, his one-eyed forever observant shipmate, playing his fiddle and teaching him the little he knew of music.

Gusta stirred him out of his reverie. 'I don't think I can have an ear for music,' she said sadly. 'I find it very difficult learning the piano and it's wearisome trying.'

'But you mustn't give up, Gusta. It can be very enjoyable and learning it helps your enjoyment of it, too.'

Gusta did not appear convinced. 'I'm joining George for cricket. I enjoy that,' she said emphatically, and hurriedly left the room.

James picked up his music sheets, feeling defeated but, on reflection, resolved to win over his pupils' appreciation of music, if only through their father's accomplished playing and enjoyment of it.

2

A fresh east wind was blowing along the Thames the next day when James took a barge from his house in Kew accompanied by his wife, Hannah, and her mother, Elisabeth, bound for Clivedon, the country residence of the prince.

'My refuge from the world,' as the prince had once confided in him.

The weekend started well, with the promise of entertainment by the prince's love of music, masques, dancing and singing, and his insistence for all his guests to join him in the ballroom. The formalities of the royal court at Leicester House did not appertain at Clivedon. The prince and his wife, Augusta, personally welcomed their guests, and their seven children ran about the house unrestricted. Servants appeared and disappeared discreetly. Food was served à la Française, allowing diners to help themselves to the buffet throughout the day.

'Oh, the choice!' exclaimed James's mother-in-law, Elisabeth, on setting eyes on it. 'Never have I seen so much food on a table.' Elisabeth could never contain her excitement.

'But you haven't dined with a future king before,' said her daughter, Hannah.

'My dear, you would be surprised whom I've dined with.'

Dishes of chicken pullets, mutton, partridge, guinea fowl, venison and grouse, perch, salmon, oysters and pies were spread in dishes with tarts, cakes, fruits, nuts, truffles and marzipan on tiered silver stands.

In the evening the prince announced that he would play his favourite pieces by Vivaldi on the cello, accompanied by his three sisters, and invited all who wished to hear them to take their seats. Amid much laughing and merriment, the men dashed for chairs to affectionately offer them to the ladies, and when calm was restored, everyone waited for the recital to begin. After the prince and his sisters had given their recital to much applause, servants returned the chairs to the walls and Princess Anne, the eldest sister of the prince, announced that the royal string quartet would play a minuet and invited everyone to dance. With one accord the guests took to the floor and, affecting graceful movements of their arms and feet, elegantly stepped and danced to the music.

Some guests looked curiously at the young coloured man dancing so harmoniously with an attractive white woman, but others took them for what they were: friends of the prince, most of whom were extraordinary too. Hannah's mother stood admiring the dancers when she became aware of a solitary gentleman standing next to her. Glancing sideways, she discerned a tall, portly figure in a grey wig and red coat. Feeling alone and desirous of attention, she discreetly let her fan fall to the floor. The man stooped down and picked it up.

'Your fan, I think, my dear,' he said, proffering it to her.

She made to take it, but his hand held on to it a little longer than necessary before releasing it. As he gave it to her, his eyes shone mischievously and she lowered hers to effect embarrassment.

'My lady, in the absence of anyone else doing so, may I introduce myself? Lord Samuel Wysop. Widower,' he added, feigning sadness before smiling engagingly. 'I noticed you from afar. A friend of the prince, madam?'

So, he had come to stand beside me deliberately and he wants me to know it, Elisabeth surmised, flushed with the thought. Having been an actress, she was used to taking the stage and did not lack confidence, but when socially required she could become affectedly modest.

'My son-in-law is the children's music teacher. He's dancing with his wife, my daughter. I'm Elisabeth, Elisabeth Butler.'

'Delighted to meet you, my dear. Have you a dancing partner? Your husband, perhaps?'

'No, my lord, I have no husband,' Elisabeth replied with a tone of regret and loss.

Her ready admission of being alone, with the insinuation that she would like it to be otherwise, made her even more interesting to Lord Wysop.

'Oh, do call me Samuel, please, if I may call you Elisabeth. Such a nice name and so apposite, if I may say so. Would you do me the honour?'

Barely waiting for an acceptance, he took her hand and they joined in the dancing, showing a familiarity with each other's movements that any observer would assume was because they were either married or long-acquainted friends.

At the end of the dance Lord Wysop invited her to join him on the balcony overlooking the garden. Elisabeth demurred sufficiently to feign modesty before graciously accepting with a smile and, taking the proffered hand of Lord Wysop, accompanied him to the balcony. The expanse of lawn leading down to the river, with the scene illuminated by a full moon, lay before them.

'Delightful,' said Lord Wysop, taking in the view and Elisabeth simultaneously. 'Am I right in presuming you to be a widow then, my dear?'

'In a sense, yes. A widow at heart. I was mistress to William Kent, you see,' replied Elisabeth, explicitly to convey her lack of artifice.

Lord Wysop raised an eyebrow at her directness. 'Ah, Kent?

Lord Burlington's protégé, and architect to the prince no less. A talented man. Never married, did he?'

'No, but we were together for over twenty years. I was with him when he died, poor man, three years ago.'

'That must have been a shock for you, my dear? Did he provide for you, may I be so bold as to ask?'

If the question had been put by a younger man, Elisabeth would have shown her distaste, but coming from this seemingly astute man, she accepted his interest with grace, although she did ask herself what his motivation was in putting the question to her. Was he interested in her for her assumed wealth or just being solicitous, she wondered?

'Oh, yes, and for my two daughters. He was a generous man.' Elisabeth's eyes moistened as she put a handkerchief to her face.

Lord Wysop took her other hand in his. 'I'm sure you meant very much to each other, my dear. Sometimes love outside of the demands of marriage can remain longer. I hope that you find comfort in happy memories of him. I know the heartache for the loss of a loved one. I was married thirty years before the good lord took my wife into his bosom, but she was suffering and it was a relief. Are both of your daughters here?'

'No, only Hannah, with her husband.' She nodded in their direction. 'He's from Jamaica. A negro, but a talented musician at Prince Frederick's court and tutor to his children. May I introduce them to you?' she said, and beckoned towards her daughter.

Hannah and James came towards them, hand in hand.

'Let me introduce Lord Wysop, whom I have just met. Lord Wysop, this is my eldest daughter, Hannah, and her husband, James.'

'I am so very delighted to meet you. A musician, I'm told. Were you born here, young man?' Lord Wysop asked, putting on an affable front.

'No, sir, I was born in the Caribbean. Jamaica. I was brought here by a sea captain.'

Lord Wysop raised an eyebrow. 'Oh, really? It would not be the late Captain Cudlip, by any coincidence, would it?'

'Why, yes, it was the same, but, sir, how come you know of him?'

'Only by name, through his son-in-law, George Hamilton. George's father was a good friend of mine. Quite remarkable,' he mused as he noticed James's long, slender hands. 'I introduced George into the House, you know, the House of Commons, but it didn't seem to do him much good. An unfortunate business. Indeed,' Lord Wysop ruminated sadly, 'it seemed to be all downhill from there for him, ending up in a debtor's prison.'

'Yes, for a little while, but he's no longer there. He's in insurance brokerage now,' said James. 'He has a desk at Lloyd's, I believe.'

'Insurance? A risky business, I hear,' retorted Lord Wysop, and, turning to Elisabeth, said, 'My business is purely one of self-indulgence since my wife passed away, but I would sacrifice it all for another wife as good.'

'May you not be long in finding her then, my lord,' said Elisabeth, smiling coquettishly over her fan.

'Thank you, my dear. How understanding of you to say so,' he replied, returning the smile. 'But do please call me Samuel. The prince forgoes formality here and I think we should follow his example. Ah, here he comes with the princess, Augusta.'

Frederick approached, inclining his head to the ladies. Even if he had not been in succession to the throne, he would have drawn attention by his long figure and affable face. 'I hope that you are all enjoying the evening. How good to see you, Lord Wysop. Thank you for speaking in the House in favour of an increase in my allowance. I do appreciate it.'

Lord Wysop lowered his head in deference. 'Your Highness, it is most regrettable that the proposal was defeated. It was well known that your father had assembled his battalions in the House to oppose it.'

'Oh, well, the dog will have its day, but I will have mine in time,' the prince said, dismissing the subject with his hand. 'Will you be umpiring tomorrow, Lord Wysop?'

'I will be happy to do so, Your Highness.'

'Good. That is agreed then. Playing with a straight bat will be testing for both teams. You know the rules we play by now and you have the authority to impose them, so there should be little argument. Is that not so? I'm told the townsmen are familiar with them and should put up a good game. I do hope the ladies will favour us with their presence.'

The ladies looked towards the princess to answer. Augusta was thirteen years younger than her husband and, like him, was long-limbed and ungainly but spoke English with a strong German accent.

'It should be very good for the children, no? We would all like to follow the game. If we understand the rules, I do not know.'

The prince turned to Augusta and spoke reassuringly. 'My dear, the players are only just getting to know the new rules themselves, but of more importance than the game, it will be another opportunity for the people to see you and for you to know them. They want to see their future queen with her family.'

'Ya, as so they do not ask me to speak. You know how my German… how do you say… intrudes, into my English?'

The prince sighed patiently. 'The more you speak English, the more you will become accustomed to it, my dear, and we must stop speaking German between ourselves; neither is it good for the children.'

Elisabeth noticed the frown on Augusta's face at the perceived rebuke. 'I think it's a most becoming accent you have, if I may say so, Your Highness,' she said.

'We all concur with that, I'm sure,' agreed Lord Wysop, flashing a smile at Elisabeth. 'And compared to the strong, guttural accent of the king, one that is more acceptable to the nation.'

The prince gave out a long sigh of despair. 'Ah, the king only speaks German in his court. I'll have none of it when I'm on the throne. I will be an English king on an English throne and only English shall be spoken.'

'You speak well, Your Highness, and the people will love you all the more for it,' said Lord Wysop patronisingly.

'That is all I seek. To reign with the approval of the people. I want them to take me to their hearts, for, I assure you, they will be in mine.'

3

All the villagers from Taplow and surroundings descended on Clivedon the following Saturday. Whether it was to see the house, a palace in all but name, or its grounds, so green and groomed, or to watch the cricket, or to see the gentry from London, or for whatever reason, their excitement pervaded the air and none were immune from its intoxication. They came on foot, by coach, boat or horse and cart, carrying bags and baskets of food and beer and claimed possession of their own plot of grass for the day by throwing down a blanket or coat to sit on. Gossip was exchanged as families and friends were reunited, babies shown off, children released from their parents' restraints and young lovers took to the seclusion of the trees. Men drifted into groups and discussed their endurance for hard work, the unpredictability of the crops, their grasping employers and the dire state of the government, but overruling all other talk were the whys and wherefores of the new rules of cricket and on which team to lay their bets.

The prince's entourage gathered together on the high terrace and chatted animatedly, aware of their privileged position and being the focus of the villager's appraisal. The ladies, fashionably dressed in white satin or silk wide-hooped gowns with jackets or robes and wearing wide-brimmed hats, moved decorously about the terrace. The men, dressed mainly in frock coats with their hair tied back or wearing wigs, circulated around the women, smiling as they pondered which to favour with their presence. The players, dressed ready for the game in white shirts and breeches, grouped around their captain, the prince, and discussed tactics for the game. He was conspicuous by his height and elegance in his red and gold embroidered cloak over his shoulders and attracted much comment from the villagers, as also did Princess Augusta, with her children tugging at her dress, remonstrating with them in a mixture of German and English.

The villagers, aware of the distance between their status, spared them no criticism and agreed how unlike the English their future king and queen appeared. A villager, pointing to James standing by the prince, called out, 'Look at the black 'un! Who be he?' and someone answered, 'An African prince, likely as not.' Then a wit said, 'A cannibal, more likely,' and everyone laughed. Another, pointing to the assembly of well-dressed guests, shouted out, 'Look at the puffed-up parasites,' but was hushed down by bystanders.

The prince handed his cloak to a servant and descended the steps with the other players to join the opposing village players waiting on the lawn. He shook hands and exchanged greetings with the village team captain, a blacksmith, who was renowned not only for being a fast and furious bowler but also for having only one eye. Lord Wysop, one of the umpires, tossed the coin for the first batting. The prince called out, 'Heads,' and, having called the toss correctly, prepared to go into first bat. The fielders leisurely took up their positions, stretched their legs in readiness and patiently waited. The blacksmith confidently strode to the wickets, feeling the ball in his hand on the way before standing behind the crease and seizing up the prince. Taking deep breaths, the blacksmith braced his shoulders, ready to bowl. The prince, standing tall and holding the bat straight and firmly in front of himself, confronted the bowler, ready for the first ball. When it came, fast and unexpectedly high, he missed it and instead took it on the chest, causing him to double up in pain and sink to the ground. As other players went to his help, the umpire called a halt to the game, and the prince, holding a hand to his chest and groaning in pain, was assisted back to the house by Lord Wysop and James, each taking an arm.

After a brief discussion, and amid murmurs from the villagers, a twelfth man was brought in and the game resumed while the prince was laid onto a chaise longue.

Augusta rushed to him and kneeled anxiously beside him. '*Danka schon, danka*,' she said, edging away the guests standing by.

'Is there a doctor here?' called out Lord Wysop.

'Yes, I'm a doctor,' a guest called out as he came forward and bent down to examine the prince. 'He's been badly bruised. We'll need to get him to bed and poultice him.'

Lord Wysop and James helped the prince to his bedroom and laid him on his bed as Augusta soothed his forehead.

'I need to go to the kitchen to make up the poultice,' said the doctor to Augusta. 'In the meantime, please have a hot towel put onto the area.'

Lord Wysop took charge and directed a servant to get the towel and hot water and another servant to go with the doctor. Despite protestations from Augusta, the prince tried to rise from the bed but gasped in agony and fell back. The doctor returned and applied the poultice and advised the prince that he must rest in bed and stay there until his personal physician arrived.

'No, I will go to Leicester House and rest there,' insisted Frederick. 'I have business to do and my physician can see me there.'

'If I may counsel Your Highness,' said the doctor, 'it would be most unwise for you to take the risk of travelling. You have a high temperature and, if I may, Your Highness, I strongly advise you to remain here resting.'

Augusta pleaded with her husband to heed the doctor's advice for all their sakes and, sighing in defeat, Frederick conceded to her request.

During the following days an abscess developed on Frederick's chest and he needed no persuading by his physician or Augusta to keep to his bed, as he felt ill and had sharp, stabbing pains in his chest. By the third day, still in pain and with a high temperature, he developed a chill and his physician was called again. Upon examination and following court practice, the doctor called for two more doctors to examine the prince. The three doctors diagnosed pleurisy and agreed that blood-letting was the remedy. Frederick reluctantly consented to the treatment and advised the princess to leave the room in case she fainted, but Augusta declined and stayed by his bedside, clasping his hand, and watched intently as a doctor punctured a vein in the prince's neck and, holding a dish, drew blood from it.

Augusta's spirits were lifted the following day when Frederick awoke and, although feeling weak, he asked for the children to be brought in. Augusta held the baby, not yet a year old, in her arms while the other seven children were ushered in with their two nurses and excitedly rushed to their father lying in bed.

'Ah, George, come and hold my hand,' he said faintly to his eldest son. 'And Gusta, you come and hold my other hand. Then everyone hold hands so I have a chain around my bed. A chain of love, my dears.

'So many happy faces,' said Frederick, smiling at each one in turn. 'All my happy children. I am so very proud of you.'

'Yes, and so is your mama, but I have something to tell you first,' said Augusta artfully to the children. 'Something that even your father does not know. Your mama is with child again! You will be having another *kleine bruder* or *schwester* next year.'

Frederick's mouth opened wide in mock astonishment and Gusta rushed to embrace her mother, saying, 'Oh, Mama, I hope it's another sister.'

George pulled a face and said, 'No. I want another brother.'

'God has been good to us, to all of us,' said the prince. 'So, children, give thanks to Him in your prayers.'

On his doctor's advice, Frederick remained in bed, but on the following night his abscess burst and the doctor was called in to dress it. Frederick coughed fitfully throughout the night with Augusta sitting beside him wiping his forehead, then with the break of dawn, he asked for George to be brought to him.

Frederick grasped his son's hand and pulled him towards himself and, breathing with difficulty, whispered to him, 'I fear I will not live to be the next king, George, but you will.' He paused for breath and, tightening his hold on his son's hand, whispered, 'Love the people and they will love you… for you were born an Englishman.'

George cried as his father groaned in agony and gasped for breath.

'*Je sens la mort*,' Frederick murmured, and, trembling violently and convulsed with spasms, lost consciousness and died.

'*Mein Gott! Nein! Nein!*' Augusta shrieked before collapsing onto him in tears.

4

James was shocked when he arrived at Leicester House the following day to find black drapes around the door and windows, the door knocker muffled, and all the curtains drawn. His unspoken question and shocked look were sufficient to bring the feared response from the footman.

'I'm sorry to tell you that His Highness has died, sir. So unexpected, it is difficult to believe. There is no visiting today, sir.'

He felt a sudden emptiness within him as he sank onto the steps and contemplated his benefactor's death; a king-in-waiting no longer. How could a life of so much promise and political ambition end so abruptly? Quietly he shed tears at the thought of Frederick's demise and the effect on Augusta and their children, now without a father who had so much to give to them, to the nation and to himself. His thoughts went to those other friends who had been so inspirational and had meant so much to him and were now dead: Captain Cudlip, Patch, William Kent and now Prince Frederick – all generous in their affection and benevolence to him. How could he ever repay such kindness?

His thoughts turned to Frederick's children. He vowed to himself that he would continue to be a part of their lives, to be there for them when they wanted him, to nurture their musical talents and to guide them whenever it was in his power to do so. In the meantime, all he could do was return home and write his condolences to Augusta and to assure her of his continued dedicated service to her and her children. The next day he read the headline news and the obituary of the prince in the *Westminster Gazette* which confirmed that the funeral would be held in Westminster Abbey and that flags would be flown at half-mast throughout the country.

James was expecting a state funeral for the prince and, accompanied by his wife and mother-in-law, each dressed sombrely in mourning clothes, he was surprised to see so few mourners in the Abbey. A tearful Princess Augusta and her seven children with two nannies occupied the front pews, but with no family members to comfort them. Neither the king nor queen nor any of the royal family was present. Their absence confirmed to James that the king's antipathy of his son was carried even to the grave, a view which was borne out the next day by comment in all the nation's newspapers with one satirising his life under the heading, 'The Prince of Wales Epigram'.

'Here lies poor Fred, who was alive and is now dead.

Had it been his sister, nobody would have missed her.

Had it been his brother, still better than another.

Had it been the whole generation, so much better for the nation.

But since it is Fred, who was alive and is now dead,

There is no more to be said!'

It was some days later, when a manservant of Princess Augusta called at James's house requesting the resumption of his attendance to her children's musical instruction at Leicester House. The house was still draped in black when he arrived and was announced to the princess, who was sitting in the drawing room surrounded by her children, wearing black. She looked frail, sad and withdrawn, her powdered face failing to hide her red-rimmed eyes. She rose absentmindedly from her chair, as though unsure why James was here, and he noticed that she was with child again.

Gathering her thoughts, she gave him a weak smile. 'Ah, James, *ja*! George 'as been asking for you to come. He must 'ave 'is music lessons again. Vill you come? Of course, ve are still in mourning and vill be for a long time, but the children… the children… their lives must continue as much as before.' She faltered and sat down again, trying to hold back her tears.

George put his arm round her. 'Mama, please. I can speak for myself. James will resume our lessons, won't you, James?'

'Yes, of course, Your Highness, as soon as you wish. There is nothing that would please me more.'

'Oh, do call me George, James, like you always have. I know Grandpapa has made me the Duke of Edinburgh now, but I am still George to my friends.'

'I want to play again,' cried Gusta. 'I know Papa would want us to continue with our music. Can we play now, James?'

'Mama, do you mind if we go to the music room?' asked George.

'*Nein*. If you wish so,' said his mother.

James took his leave of the princess and followed the children to the music room where they soon resumed their practise. As he sat listening to their scrapings on their cellos, his thoughts turned to rumours circulating the court: that the king had asked to take George, now the heir apparent, into his care and that Augusta had stubbornly refused the king's offer; also that Frederick had spent beyond his means and had left the princess with large debts. Certainly, James knew that money was owed to him and that he had not received his stipend for many months.

He waited until George put aside his cello and asked him tentatively, 'May I put a question to you, George? Will you be staying here now, with your mother?'

'That's two questions, James, not one,' replied George, true to his pedantic nature. 'Yes, I will be staying with Mama. Grandpapa has agreed to it, and yes, we will be staying here, although Mama says that Grandpapa would like me to live in the palace. It is Mama's wish and it is mine too, that I stay with her and my brothers and sisters. How else could I look after them, as I promised to Papa?'

James thought how mature and ready for responsibility the fourteen-year-old boy had become. 'That is a very commendable promise and one which I am sure is in your nature to keep,' he complimented, certain of the boy's earnestness.

'Thank you, James. Lord Wysop said much the same. Mama has agreed too, for him to guide me in his principles for living a good life and to supervise my education. She says he is an admirable man to follow Papa and would be a trusted friend and advisor. Of course, I will always be indebted to you, James, for your guidance and instruction, and I hope we will keep our friendship.'

'I hope I will be worthy of it, George, thank you.'

It was of little surprise to James to hear of Lord Wysop being spoken of with such favour, as he had been a close friend of Frederick's and, as well as tabling a motion in Parliament to increase the prince's allowance, they had played cricket together and shared an interest in botany. Nevertheless, thought James, as he took his leave, it was apparent that Lord Wysop was not only ingratiating himself with the young heir apparent but also with his widowed mother.

On his departure from the house, which was, as his usual habit, through the side door, he was surprised to encounter Lord Wysop arriving at the same door.

'Saw you at the Abbey,' Lord Wysop said hurriedly, looking flushed. 'Never spoke… wasn't appropriate… shocking business… just paying my respects.'

James wondered why the lord looked so embarrassed and had

apologised to him and thought it may be due to their meeting again at the servants' entrance, but his haste, brief words and apparent embarrassment made James wonder.

5

James arrived home to find his wife waiting for him. Standing up, she embraced him and looked into his eyes. 'I'm with child, my dear,' she announced joyfully.

James held her and kissed her. 'Oh, Hannah, that is wonderful. Are you sure?'

'Yes, I think so. I've been to see my mother and she thinks so, too. I was sick during the night and I feel changes in me that I've not had before.'

'Tell me what I can do?' asked James excitedly.

Hannah smiled at his reaction. 'There is nothing for you to do yet, James. In time, yes, but it will be months before the child is born. We must be patient.'

'Take care not to exert yourself, Hannah. Don't lift anything heavy and tell me when you feel unwell.'

'I shall continue as always for now, James. It's too soon to start restricting my life. Mother said that she never let my birth or my sister's stop her from acting.'

'That I can believe,' said James unkindly.

Hannah's voice dropped to a whisper. 'She confided in me that Lord Wysop was calling on her.'

'Then surely she must be encouraging him? Lord Wysop

indeed! He seems to be a very busy gallant. I just met him going into Leicester House, by the servants' entrance, would you know? Unlike a lord, I thought, to avoid attention. The princess speaks very highly of him and I know that George is also greatly imbued with his affection.'

'I think my mother is in love with him. You are not suggesting that he is making love with the Princess Augusta as well, are you?'

'He's a very handsome man and if he has desires on your mother, why not Augusta too? She has much more to offer.'

'Oh, James, how unkind! He cannot be paying court to two women at once, surely?'

'He wouldn't be the first man to do so.'

'Then I must warn my mother before she gets hurt. You know how emotional she is and living on her own now makes her very vulnerable to suitors.'

'Well, we have no facts to go on, and perhaps I misjudge him. He's been a good friend to me, so I wouldn't mention it to your mother. You may only cause her unnecessary pain.'

Hannah's mother, Elisabeth, was soon made aware of Lord Wysop's attachment to the princess, but it was not from her daughter. A scurrilous pamphlet was anonymously published, reporting that Lord Wysop, "who was renowned for his fine pair of legs, was using them to jump into bed with the princess". The pamphlet had wide distribution in London and Elisabeth's friends could not bring it to her attention quickly enough.

When Hannah visited her mother, she found her distraught and embittered.

'He held out such promise to me. He even spoke of marriage,' she cried. 'I knew Samuel was friendly with the princess, of course, but I assumed that was because of his friendship with Prince Frederick.'

'Mother, you do not know if the report is true.'

'We've been corresponding to each other every day when we didn't meet, but my last three letters have gone unanswered. For whatever other reason would he have stopped, I ask?'

'James sees him sometimes at Leicester House. Would you wish James to make a discreet enquiry to him on your behalf? He would do it with the most delicacy, I'm sure.'

'I'm not sure that I want James to be my go-between.'

'He is your son-in-law and, as such, I'm sure he would agree that he has a responsibility for your welfare. He would be very tactful, Mother.'

'I don't think Samuel would take kindly to his interference. I'll give Samuel a few more days and then, if he doesn't call on me or write, I will consider James raising a polite question with him.'

'I'm sure there is an explanation, Mother.'

It was more than a few days before James saw Lord Wysop at Leicester House, when James was in the music room with George and a manservant announced that Lord Wysop had urgent business with the prince and would like to see him. George said to show the lord in immediately and intimated to James to remain.

'Your Highness,' began Lord Wysop, after looking askance at James, 'I have news for you alone, sir, that is not for the ears of servants.'

'Oh, come, Samuel, you know that James is almost a family member and hardly a servant. What have you to tell me?'

Lord Wysop pursed his lips in hesitation before answering. 'It will be public knowledge soon enough, Your Highness, but, before it is, you must be told privately,' he said persistently.

Putting on a look of tolerance, George turned to James, who was already turning to leave. 'Well, James, I'm sorry, but you are excused.'

The lord waited for the door to close behind James. 'I have received private information that the king will be asking for your attendance at the court for you to be made the Prince of Wales, Your Highness, as is your right.'

'Oh, no! Prince of Wales already? Does my mother know?'

'Not to my knowledge, Your Highness, but I will call on her

and let her know in confidence. There is one other matter you should know, Your Highness. The king will expect you to move into St James's Palace, always the grand establishment of the princes of Wales.'

'Then you must tell my mother that, too.'

'That I will do immediately.'

Lord Wysop made his way to Augusta's apartments and, after asking her footman, was announced and entered her rooms, whereupon he kissed her hand with great solemnity.

'My dear princess, I have heard that the king has decided to make George the Prince of Wales immediately. He will be asking for your attendance at court, and for George's, to agree to it before making the announcement.'

Augusta frowned disapprovingly. 'Why now? I do not think so. He's too young.'

'I do not think you can refuse the king, my dear. It is only to be expected and, if it was delayed, it would only lead to conjecture and rumour. However, you may not realise that St James's Palace is the residence of the Prince of Wales and the king will expect him to follow protocol and establish his court there.'

'What? Take George from me? No, I will not agree to that. Not at his age. He would come under the influence of the king and he's my ward, my son! I'll bring him up to honour his father. We know the king would never do that!'

Lord Wysop nodded in agreement. 'Then you must stand firm, my dear, for I share your concerns. George is responding very well under my guidance. I suggest that you advise George to accept his new title with gratitude, but it is for you to persuade the king to agree for George to continue to live here. Tell the king you want George to grow up with his brothers and sisters, for he takes his responsibilities towards them to his heart.'

Augusta dabbed the tears welling from her eyes. 'Of course, he may say that I could live there with George, and his brothers and sisters, but I don't wish him to. Too many bad influences on him there. *Nein!* I will not have it.'

Lord Wysop held her hand protectively. 'Very wise, my dear. George will learn his moral values from you by example, and from me by my instruction of them. I have already started him on a course of lectures on natural philosophy and, if I may say so, he is responding very well to my tuition.'

'I know George values your instruction very much, Samuel, and the more time you spend with him, the more earnest he becomes in his application,' responded Augusta.

Lord Wysop smiled in acknowledgement. 'Of course, Augusta, but there are influences here which I do not entirely concur with. His music master, James, for one. Neither his background nor his race suit that required of a tutor for a future king.'

Augusta looked down reflectively. 'Frederick introduced James and valued him very highly, but I think it was more his exoticism which Frederick thought would add to George's knowledge of the world. George would take it very badly if James was to be dismissed, as indeed would the other children, I'm sure.'

Lord Wysop raised an eyebrow in apprehension. 'Yes, the children do appear to have an unnatural attraction towards him, but is that something we want to encourage? I don't think so, my dear.'

Lord Wysop relaxed in his chair and stretched out his legs. His thoughts turned to the evening at Clivedon when Elisabeth introduced James to him. That had been his first meeting with Elisabeth too, he contemplated. How he had succumbed to her enticements that night, a night to remember or, perhaps, better to forget. The scandal-mongers would love to besmirch him with that dalliance if it became known – an actress, no less! He had cut her out of his life now and the last thing he wanted was her negro son-in-law as a court favourite.

'There are a number of highly talented music masters in London who would exceed James's talents, by far. Mr Handel for one, I'm sure.'

Augusta was reluctant to overturn a decision of her late husband but felt assured by the confidence of Lord Wysop and his earnestness in looking after her interests. 'I hear that Mr Handel has too much self-esteem to be beholden to anyone, but I agree that a replacement for James could soon be found. I doubt that George will agree to it, but I will bring it up with him carefully,' she said.

Lord Wysop stood up and pressed her hand in gentle affection. 'George will follow your advice, my dear, as I'm sure he does in all matters.'

Augusta laid her other hand onto his. 'Only if you agree, Samuel. You know he values your advice before all others.'

Samuel smiled in acknowledgement of the compliment, perceiving it as the truth, but decided that a degree of modesty would not be out of place. 'My lady, you flatter me exceedingly.'

Augusta looked at his handsome, elegant figure and felt the loneliness of her widowhood and suddenly longed for the comfort and support of a man's arms again. As she arose to leave the room, she hesitated before giving voice to her thoughts. 'Then you may flatter me with your company tonight, Samuel.'

Lord Wysop took her hand and tenderly kissed her lips. Augusta returned the kiss modestly at first then, consumed by her need for love, she kissed him passionately as he embraced her.

6

Elisabeth's remorse at not hearing from Lord Wysop, when a few days extended into two weeks, weighed heavily on her mind. As mistress of the late William Kent, she was well used to circumspection and anonymity, but now she felt that she had been spurned and was consumed with anger.

'I'll call on him in his mansion and demand to see him,' she said to her daughter. 'Or I will raise the roof and all of London will know about it.'

'Mother, it would only rebound on you. Don't do anything that would raise a scandal. Let James speak to him.'

On his next visit to Leicester House, James again encountered Lord Wysop and, despite the lord's previous hostility, James greeted him warmly, enquiring after his health. The lord's response was cold and reserved but, nevertheless, James attempted to be cordial.

'My mother-in-law, Elisabeth Butler, has asked me to give you her respects and enquires about your health, my lord. She hopes that, in the absence of correspondence from you, she can be reassured of your continued friendship.'

'Oh, I've been busy. I have much to do here. The matters of the late prince require my attention.'

'And your relationship with Elisabeth? Does not that require some attention, sir? She is most distraught at not hearing from you.'

The lord braced himself in defiance. 'Relationship? Relationship? What are you insinuating, man? If she claims relationship with me, then the woman is demented, and you, sir, I'll have you summoned for spreading false rumours and dishonouring my reputation. Do not lecture me, young man. Remember your position in this court, for you may not hold on to it much longer.'

As Lord Wysop stormed off, James felt weakened at the threat but resolved not to be intimidated by it and continued to the music room, where he found George alone and already practising on the cello. When James suggested that they resumed his instruction, George showed a reluctance to do so and continued his practise until he had finished the piece.

'H'm, h'm.' George hesitated as if he was unsure whether to speak. 'Mother has been questioning me about you, James. She thinks that some other tutor may improve my application to music. She says that you are too loath to correct my errors, that you are too much of a friend, James, and not enough of a teacher. What do you make of that, what?'

James was taken aback but sensed that George's mother was reiterating Lord Wysop's objections. 'I'm sorry to hear of it, but I don't think being a friend excludes me from being a good teacher. I have no reserve on your musical instruction, George, and if your mother thinks you could benefit from another teacher, then she may be right.'

'But I do not want another tutor, James. It will not happen. I shall apply myself most diligently to my music and practise more. You will see. I will not bear unjustified criticism of your instruction.'

'Thank you for your faith in me, but I feel that your mother may be prevailed upon by another who does not share your views.'

'Another? If you mean Lord Wysop, James, you know I have the greatest respect for him and he has nothing but my best interests at heart. There may be some misunderstanding between you both, but he has made no criticism of you to me, James, and I feel it would be unjustified if he did.'

George was being disingenuous, as his mother had already told him of Lord Wysop's reservations, which he had derided. Now, he recalled his father's maxim that the man who told a king what he did not want to hear must, because of it, be a trustworthy friend. Could it be, George asked himself, that Lord Wysop was that friend? He put the thought aside for now.

'Now that summer is here, James, we shall be moving to the Kew House next week and I shall expect our lessons to continue there, as usual, James. I look forward to the fresh air of Kew.'

'I always look forward to the move, if only because I can walk there from my home,' replied James.

On his return home, James found his mother-in-law, Elisabeth, in an emotional argument with his wife, before she turned to him. 'Did you speak to Lord Wysop on my behalf?' she asked, slightly scornfully.

'Yes, I did broach the subject, but, of course, he denied that he had any relationship with you and furthermore threatened me for slandering him. It was a heated exchange and I think it would be unwise of you or me to pursue it further.'

Elisabeth sank into the chair and started sobbing. 'He's spurned my love,' she kept repeating between tears. 'It will out! It will out! I won't shame myself now, but my day will come and I'll have my revenge. He will know I'm no weak and feeble woman.'

'Elisabeth, don't upset yourself so. Don't inflame his anger and you won't have to suffer it.'

Hannah eventually pacified her mother by bringing in her own concerns of her imminent childbirth. Her fears and anxieties were increasing as her time drew near and she felt the pains and unease in her body. She foresaw a dark cloud looming and neither

her mother nor her husband's loving care could dispel her fears.

'If I should die, will you look after my baby?' she asked of her mother.

'Why ever should you say that? You'll not die! I'll be here for you and the baby and so will the midwife, my dear. Don't worry, your fear is unnecessary but not unusual for your first child, you will see.'

Throughout her pregnancy Hannah had excessive bleeding and lapsed into sadness and periods of crying which reassurances from her mother failed to quell. Eight months into her pregnancy, James sought the advice of his friend, Dr Lucas, and took a boat to the Strand where the doctor lived with Susie, his wife, above her coffee shop.

Following discussion between them, Dr Lucas agreed to return to Kew with James, and after questioning and examining Hannah he could find nothing wrong but offered to be on hand and oversee the midwife at the birth and, despite the disagreement from Elisabeth, advised Hannah to remain as active as possible.

Elisabeth protested further when Dr Lucas said he wanted the bedroom to be bright and airy with the window open to ward off any infection in the room.

'Airy?' she questioned. 'It's well known that draughts should be avoided. Why, I had the keyholes blocked up and the curtains drawn when I was giving birth!'

Dr Lucas gave her a patient look. 'Then, my dear, you were fortunate indeed to give birth to such healthy daughters. Now we know better. Air should be passing through the room, freeing it from the bad odours and vapours and avoiding infection.' He turned to James. 'Be advised, James, keep the room as fresh as possible and encourage your wife to get up and about. I will be here when the contractions begin if accommodation can be made for me beforehand, please.'

Hannah's apprehension increased at the disagreement between the doctor and her mother and she became overwhelmed by grief, sobbing when her mother told her that the midwife had said that she would not be attending if she was expected to follow the doctor's strictures.

'I'll be here for you, Hannah, and see you come to no harm. I brought you and your sister into the world. He may be a doctor, but he's not had my experience.'

It was at midnight amid a thunderstorm when Hannah's labour pains started and James, going against his mother-in-law's objections, ordered a coach for the doctor to be sent for. When the doctor arrived some four hours later Hannah was writhing in agony and being comforted by her mother. In the half light of daybreak, the candles were still lit and with the curtains still drawn, a stale smell pervaded the airless room.

'I'll have the curtains and window opened, please, and there's no need for the candles now,' said the doctor defiantly to Elisabeth. 'She needs air.'

'Not draughts she doesn't. Be it on your head, but I don't think it's wise,' she replied before resentfully complying with his wishes. 'It will be a slow labour, I think,' she said, and turned to the servant. 'Fill up the pans with water and have them ready.'

The doctor nodded in agreement. 'Yes, I suspect that may be so, being her first birth.'

James and Elisabeth exchanged concerned looks as a wind blew through the room and Hannah's moaning increased.

'It could be hours yet,' her mother said, putting an arm under her daughter's head and mopping her brow.

Time passed slowly with intermittent screams and cries of anguish from Hannah, with her mother and the doctor on each side of the bed consoling her and James looking on helplessly. Hannah's cries turned into a scream.

'It's coming,' said the doctor as he eased Hannah into position to deliver the baby. Eventually the head of the baby emerged, and the doctor brought the red, wrinkled body out and cut the umbilical cord.

‘A boy, a beautiful boy,’ he said, tenderly wiping the baby before handing him over to Elisabeth.

James embraced his wife and kissed her. ‘How wonderful! We have a boy. How do you feel, my dear?’

‘Is he alright?’

‘Yes, Hannah, he’s a lovely baby,’ said her mother, handing the baby gently back to her. ‘Take him in your arms now and nurse him. Then you must rest.’

‘What name shall we give him?’ asked Hannah.

‘I would like him to be called Henry, after the captain. Henry Cudlip the second,’ said James.

‘Yes, we’ll call him Henry. Annabelle and Felicity will be very happy,’ agreed Hannah.

Hannah nursed her baby all that morning before falling asleep. She awoke trembling, feeling alternatively hot and cold, and a fever developed during the night. In the morning, as James tried to soothe her, she slipped in and out of consciousness, crying in pain and desperation. When the doctor returned, the fever had intensified and Elisabeth was feeding the baby with a bottle. Hannah was vomiting and perspiring profusely, complaining of stomach pains and of being hot and thirsty. Dr Lucas suspected that she had puerperal fever, which often followed a birth, and made up a sleeping potion for her. Hannah suffered for two more days before she lost consciousness during the night and, emitting a long last gasp, gave her last breath in James’s arms. Elisabeth screamed in grief as James wept over his wife’s body.

Dr Lucas induced Elisabeth to take a sedative, despite her protestations and vitriolic criticism of him, and with the help of James carried her to bed. He did his best to comfort James, but to little effect. He felt sorely grieved that he had failed to sustain Hannah’s life and, conscious of his responsibility, passed a sleepless night sitting in a chair by her bedside.

Next morning, Elisabeth confronted him in a rage of despair and anguish. ‘A doctor, you claim to be? See what you’ve done!

You've killed my daughter! Killed her with your draughts and your airy room! You claim the fever killed her? No! You did it! You killed her!'

7

The church of St Anne's on Kew Green was filled with mourners for the funeral of Hannah with some villagers standing at the back, as James and his mother-in-law, Elisabeth, walked slowly behind the coffin to the altar. As heads turned, James could discern Annabelle and Felicity, the daughters of his former owner, Captain Cudlip, with their husbands, Francis and George, all looking compassionately at him; his friends, Dr Lucas and Susie, looking distraught, as were his friends from Chiswick, William Hogarth and his wife, Jane. Standing apart, were Lord and Lady Burlington, who had known of Hannah as the illegitimate daughter of their protégé and architect, the late William Kent.

James unconsciously took the scene in, but in truth, he could hardly believe it as he followed the white lily-draped coffin. He had cried throughout the long nights since her death and had dreamt of her when sleep overtook him, only to awaken to the horrible reality of her death and now felt that he had no more tears. He was vaguely aware of the minister delivering his eulogy, of the prayers and the hymn-singing and the many sympathetic looks. As he walked back down the aisle and to the graveyard where the newly dug grave awaited his wife's body, his mind rejected what his eyes saw but he was aware of Elisabeth and her other daughter,

Caroline, standing beside him, looking into the grave and crying uncontrollably. Suddenly Caroline fainted and almost collapsed into the grave, arousing him from his reverie. Men rushed with their arms outstretched towards Caroline when Elisabeth cried out, 'Keep off her! Don't you touch her!'

Her cry was directed at Dr Lucas, who had been the first to step forward, but everyone stood still, embarrassed by the outcry and momentarily immobilised by it, until James stooped to lift Caroline up and Francis came to his help and carried her back into the church accompanied by Elisabeth, angry and distraught.

Dr Lucas looked humiliated as the minister waited and the bearers rested the coffin on the ground. Everyone stood silent at the graveside wondering why Elisabeth's objection had been directed at the doctor and in a so vehement and unconstrained manner. After five minutes James returned, looking calm and dignified, apologised to the gathering and asked the minister to continue the burial as Elisabeth would remain with her daughter Caroline before they took a carriage home.

After the minister said a prayer, the coffin was lowered into the grave and a mourner stepped forward and dropped rosemary sprigs onto it. James, controlling his emotions, scattered a handful of earth on top and, maintaining his composure, with head bowed, returned in silence to the church with the minister.

Carriages took invited mourners to James's house where, over biscuits and wine, the talk turned to Elisabeth's outburst. Dr Lucas profusely apologised to James for being the cause of it, but before James could exonerate him from blame, they were joined by William Hogarth and his wife, Jane, expressing their condolences.

William, however, soon appeared to be more interested in the gossip and to learn about "Young Prince George" and his mother Augusta and of any "goings-on" at their residence.

'Did James know if Lord Wysop was a frequent visitor?' he asked brazenly. 'Did James know that Lord Wysop had bought a house on Kew Green to be near the princess? Was it true that young George was a bit slow on the uptake as people said?'

'Why, no! George is as bright as a new penny but much wiser,' said James.

James diplomatically evaded the questions on Lord Wysop as he was worried that William would use any knowledge gained to deride the lord and the royals in his satires, and instead, turned the conversation to William's support for the Foundling Hospital before they were joined by Lord and Lady Burlington.

'Ah! Mr Hogarth!' Lord Burlington exclaimed, confronting him. 'Considering that we both have houses in Chiswick, we see very little of each other.'

'Well, yes, but we do move in different circles and I have only a very small house, my lord,' said Mr Hogarth, affecting an obsequious manner. 'You have your architecture and Grand Tours, and I have my sketchings, and London gives me all I need.'

Lord Burlington put on a smile. 'Then we are both fortunate indeed, Mr Hogarth. I do admire your satires and I have never before had the opportunity to thank you for your *Burlington Gate* satire as the way to taste in art,' he added sardonically.

'The popularity of the print is reward enough, my lord. I don't look for any other approval, my lord,' Mr Hogarth replied tetchily.

'It's not for the money, then? I am so glad,' said Lord Burlington with continued irony. 'Burlington House has not come under so much scrutiny since the publication. It is veritably impossible to get out of the gates for the crowds on some days, indeed, let alone get into them.'

Lady Burlington rested her hand on her husband's arm as if to restrain him and, turning her back on Mr Hogarth, turned to James. 'James, you would not think listening to these two that we are here to express our sadness at your grievous loss. You have our deepest sympathy. Perhaps, in time, after your mourning, you may wish to consider giving a recital at Chiswick House. You might consider having it in memory of your dear wife.'

'That is very kind of you. Yes, I will most certainly consider it, my lady. Thank you for your commiseration.'

They were joined by Annabelle and her sister with their husbands, each expressing their sympathy and asking about Henry, the baby.

'Elisabeth has him in her care and has engaged a wet nurse,' explained James. 'She will look after him.'

'We would be very happy to have him, James,' said Annabelle. 'You know we don't have any children of our own and he would have all our love and care. He would be more accessible to you, living so near to us. I would love to have him, and to bring him up, and he would always know you as his father.'

'Yes, I will consider it, but Elisabeth is his grandmother and already has a great affection for him, although,' James added after reflection, 'she may be induced into parting with him as she does have other affiliations.'

His own response made him consider. He had given little thought to the baby since the birth, glad that his mother-in-law had taken responsibility for him. Perhaps, he thought, considering her emotional state and her vicissitudes, he had been too ready to pass him onto her, and wouldn't Annabelle give his child a better and more stable an upbringing? Annabelle had been like an older sister since her father had brought him here, giving him a home and his name. He had grown up under her care, and had she not inspired her father to cast off his chains of slavery? What better mother could his child have than Annabelle if he couldn't have Hannah?

His thoughts were interrupted by a touch on his arm by Susie, standing with her husband. He had always known Thomas as a man of principle and strong opponent of slavery, and whom he still had to believe in, despite his failure to save Hannah's life and Elisabeth's condemnation of him.

'James, I hope that your despair will not turn you from our friendship,' said Dr Lucas. 'I know that Elisabeth will never forgive me, but please don't you hold me responsible. What I did was what I knew to be right for the birth and it did not contribute to your wife's death, believe me, James. It was the fever, puerperal fever. I have since been doing some further research on it and the symptoms your wife showed confirmed it to me. There is no cure for it, James. Nevertheless, I'm contrite to think that it could be misinterpreted by Elisabeth. Susie and I have the greatest admiration for you, James, and we value your friendship. We hope that you will honour us with a visit when you are able. We have much to discuss with you.'

Susie embraced him affectionately before clasping his hands. 'James, come and support us in our cause. You and I have so much in common. We've been very fortunate, but we must not forget the slaves we left behind, our brothers and sisters. We must continue to fight for their emancipation, James. Thomas and I have regular meetings in our coffee house and more people come now, even some politicians. Do come and join us, James.'

'Yes, I must take the cause up again. I've been too comfortable in my own world and have shut out the injustices. Thank you for reminding me, Susie.'

James's servant came forward and, after excusing himself, said that a servant of Elisabeth's had arrived and had been instructed, with the approval of James, to read out an announcement on Elisabeth's behalf. James agreed for him to speak.

'Ladies and gentlemen. My lady, Elisabeth Butler, has asked me to read out to you the following apology. She sends her deepest regrets for her absence and her unintended departure from the burial of her daughter, which was provoked by the presence of Dr Lucas and due to the strain and grief at the loss of her daughter, for which she still holds Dr Lucas responsible. She notes that, as her accusation is a private matter, she would not wish it to be reported to newspapers.'

James turned to a very embarrassed Dr Lucas. 'I am sorry. I had no idea what was going to be said.'

'James, it is not your fault. She is very distressed and only time will alleviate it. I wish to make an announcement in answer to the accusation, if I may.'

James hushed for silence and asked for everyone's attention as the doctor cleared his throat.

'Ladies and gentlemen. I ask for your courtesy in allowing me to respond to the unexpected accusation you have just heard read out. I most vehemently deny the accusation that I was responsible for the death of Hannah, whom I knew as a friend as well as being her doctor over many years and whose death I deeply mourn. Her death was caused by puerperal fever, the contagion of which is as yet unknown but is suspected of being of foul and obnoxious airs being breathed in during pregnancy. It was in this belief – nay, knowledge – that I requested the windows to be opened for fresh air to be circulated in the birthing chamber. I regret the distress caused and felt by her mother, which I fully understand and commiserate with, but must refute the accusation that my actions in any way contributed to the death of Hannah.'

The question passed through Dr Lucas's mind that by Elisabeth asking those present not to report her accusation to the newspapers, she had intentionally planted the seed to do so, thereby ensuring that someone so disposed would, possibly out of malice, report it. Being sensational, a London paper would report it only too readily to pillory his professional reputation and, by imputation, his campaign for the abolishment of slavery. Was this Elisabeth's intention and her revenge, he asked himself?

Dr Lucas's suspicion was soon confirmed when, two days later, the *Gazetteer* and the *London Daily Advertiser* printed the story on the front page under the headline:

"**Actress Accuses Doctor Death**"

and then continued:

'**Stage actress** Miss **Elisabeth Butler**, former **Mistress** and **Heiress** of the late architect **William Kent**, **accused Dr Thomas Lucas, MD**, of the killing of her **daughter**, **Hannah**, by unwisely ventilating the birth chamber during his delivery of the child's birth. **Miss Butler** made the **accusation**, which was read out to all the **mourners** following the **burial** of her daughter. In an interview with this newspaper, **Miss Butler** said that the doctor **opened the windows and the doors** to the room, thereby causing cold and draughts to weaken her daughter in childbirth and led to her **death**, disregarding her strong **protestations** and her own experience of having given birth to two daughters.

'We have tried unsuccessfully to contact the **accused doctor**, but two doctors whom we have consulted advise that birthing chambers should be kept warm and free from draughts to avoid **cold** and **fever infecting the mother or child**.'

Dr Lucas feared the weight of public censure would be against him and demanded that a reply to the accusation exonerating him from guilt be printed on the front page. The newspaper accepted his right to reply but printed it discreetly on an inside page. He knew that he would not win a public argument against a mother mourning the death of a daughter and therefore decided not to pursue the slander any further, hoping that time itself would expunge the accusation. He had underestimated the tenacity of a revengeful, bereaved mother.

8

James's residency in the village of Kew was well established, although he had little knowledge of its other inhabitants, but following the death of his wife and the consequent accusation made in the London paper, many friendly villagers approached him offering their sympathies. He realised then that he was more accepted by society than he had thought, despite his colour. Who it was that had reported the incident to the London paper was never revealed, but James did not exclude Elisabeth herself from the possibility. He knew her to be a very determined woman, one who never forgave a perceived injustice or forgot a grievance, real or imagined. Having set her face for revenge against Lord Wysop after his rejection of her, James remembered that she had boasted to him that her day would come.

Elisabeth also talked of returning to her own house. She obviously did not see her role as being the attentive grandmother of a half-cast motherless baby or as housekeeper for a young, coloured son-in-law, whatever his musical accomplishments were, and vehemently objected when James refused to disassociate himself from Dr Lucas. She returned to her house in Covent Garden, avid to resume her social life, free to visit the opera, the theatre or stroll in the Ranelagh Gardens; but with revenge still simmering in her heart, she remained vowed to expose her deceiver, Lord Wysop.

Her satisfaction in publicising her denunciation of Dr Lucas in the London paper led her to try a similar exposure of the lord, which the paper readily agreed to publish in competition to a story of Lord Wysop and Princess Augusta already circulating in pamphlets in London.

The paper blazoned the story on the front page with appropriate highlights.

> "**Actress Accuses Lord of Deceit**"
>
> '**Lord Wysop**, already **renowned "for his fine pair of legs"**, which he is reported to use to good effect in a **royal bedchamber**, has been **accused** by **Miss Elisabeth Butler**, the popular **London actress**, of **deceiving** her while consorting with a **Royal Personage**. **Miss Butler**, former **mistress** of the late **William Kent**, architect and friend of **Lord Burlington**, states that she and **Lord Wysop** were in a **loving relationship** while he was plying court at **Princess Augusta's Court**!
>
> 'Whilst we cannot **verify the accuracy** of this allegation (as readers will understand, we do not have access to the **bedchambers**) it does follow **anonymous reports** in pamphlets, which we disassociate this newspaper from, of **Lord Wysop's close friendship** with **Princess Augusta**, widow of the late **Prince Frederick**.'

Elisabeth held her head high that evening when she strolled in the fashionable Ranelagh Gardens with her second daughter, Caroline, as companion, aware that she was attracting more looks and whispered comments from other strollers than usual and not a few were from gentlemen. Some, known to her, acknowledged her with a bow, intent on conversation, and the ones she deigned to speak to complimented her on her exposure of Lord Wysop, but she knew in her heart that in his place they would probably behave in the same way. Some of the ladies she stopped to talk to praised her for being so outspoken and sympathised with her on men's treachery, but she suspected that, behind their fans, scornful remarks would be shared with their companions.

Lord Wysop nearly suffered apoplexy when he read the exposure, but after a long period of deliberation, he resolved not to respond to the report as to do so would only incur further interest and attacks. Far better, he reasoned, to let the accusation whither on the vine of silence and instead get his retribution by other means.

On his following visit to Princess Augusta, he again raised his objection to James's tutorage of Prince George to her.

'When George is king, he will be open to ridicule by having an ex-slave as his music tutor and you, too, my dear, will suffer for it. Better to take the axe now and disassociate James entirely from your court. You must realise that it is in the long-term interests of George, my dear.'

Augusta sighed. She was reluctant to make a decision before it was necessary. 'Yes, I can see the virtue in what you suggest, but it's likely to be years before George is king. By then he will not need a tutor.'

Lord Wysop had thought of the long-term consequences both for George and for himself. He viewed their relationship as mutually beneficial to them both and tied his political ambitions to George becoming king.

'But you are his guardian now and will be criticised for his association with the Negro cause. Think of the damage that could do to the crown, my dear.'

'I allow that I would not wish for George or myself to become entangled in the slave argument.' The princess hesitated before conceding, 'Yes, I will speak to George.'

'Thank you, my dear. I will back you up in my advice to him,' replied Lord Wysop.

After dinner that evening when the younger children had been put to bed, she sat with her three eldest children, George, Gusta and Edward, in conversation, as was her habit, and brought up the subject of their musical education.

'I think it would do you all good to have a change of music tutor. James has taught you all he can now. You must have a wider knowledge which would come by a change of tutor. I know, only too well, how difficult it is to cut yourself off from the past, but we must look to your futures, and sometimes it is necessary to accept change.'

The children all looked downcast.

'But we know James and we all like him,' protested George. 'He never stops teaching us. He always says that we have more to learn. Is it that we have not been practising enough? He always tells us that, but, if that is so, then we will practise more, won't we?'

Gusta and Edward nodded eagerly in agreement.

'Is it, perhaps, you think that he doesn't discipline us enough?' asked Gusta. 'But he does, Mama, he does.'

'Well, I'm glad to hear it, but it is not that. No, it is to give you the benefit of a different experience with a different tutor. Besides, Lord Wysop agrees with me. You know he has your interests at heart.'

'Yes, Mama, he is always telling me so,' said George sardonically. 'Anyway, being my tutor is one thing, but being a friend is another, and James will always be my friend and I will not stop seeing him.'

'And neither will I,' agreed Gusta. 'I want to go to his concerts, whether he teaches us or not.'

'Or me,' said Edward. 'He's the only black friend I have and he's had adventures. I never have adventures.'

George looked up earnestly at his mother, sensing that she had more bad news. 'We shall see James on our next lesson, won't we?' he asked petulantly.

'Yes, perhaps for a few more lessons until Lord Wysop has engaged his replacement,' replied Augusta.

The next day, Augusta told Lord Wysop that the children had been advised of James's dismissal and asked him not to rush it but to give the children time to make the adjustment. However, Lord Wysop lost no time in summoning James to tell him that his services as tutor of music at the court would shortly be no longer required.

James took the sad news in silence, but his face showed his concern.

Lord Wysop appeared disinclined to give any reason for his dismissal.

'Has the princess advised you to do this? Do the children know?' James finally asked.

Lord Wysop glared at James on being questioned. 'I will have you know that I advised the princess and yes, the children have been told. Their mother has already explained it to them and they have accepted it.'

'Then give me your reasons for my dismissal.'

The lord looked outraged. 'I am not obliged to answer to you, but I'll have you know, your colour, sir, and your origins, are prejudicial to your tutorage of a future king.'

'A future king may be more enlightened than a past one,' said James after some deliberation.

'Ah! Do I detect a criticism of His Majesty? Your comment is bordering on treason, young man. Is this the disloyalty you teach to George?'

'No, sir, I teach music, not politics, and I may remind you that I have received no payment for my teaching for more than two years and would expect some recompense for my duties.'

'Recompense? Recompense? The devil you do! Such impertinence! Is it not enough that you, a black man, have been privileged to teach royal children?' the lord lambasted.

'I will expect you to honour the agreement I had with Prince Frederick and settle that, sir.'

'Then, sir, join the procession for the settlement of Frederick's debts. You will be waiting a very long time, and while you are waiting in vain, thank that damned mother-in-law of yours for your situation,' said Lord Wysop, and added with scorn, 'or the loss of one!'

9

James stood by the river bank, with Kew village behind him, watching herons waiting patiently for unsuspecting fish to swim into their orbit, and the similarity of this with Lord Wysop came to his mind as he pictured Lord Wysop as the heron and himself as the fish, caught in the net of a very influential and vengeful lord. Two ferry boats were carrying passengers and passing each other in the middle of the fast-flowing river. Beyond the far bank he could see the village of Chiswick and the house where Captain Cudlip had first brought him eighteen years ago. In his mind's eye, he recalled the captain standing on the shoreline and pointing to the house, shouting, 'Welcome to Jamaica House, lad,' and Patch stumbling towards them with his arm outstretched, shouting, 'Captain! Smiley! Welcome home.' The name the captain called him resounded in his mind as the vision faded away.

Now with his infant son being brought up in the same house by the captain's daughter, James reflected on the unpredictability of life and, not for the first time, questioned whether he had done the right thing to hand over his child. He had made the decision in his grief and mourning of the death of his wife, but was it right for him to relinquish his responsibility of their child? He had thought it to be in the child's own interest to have a surrogate mother, one as good and loving as Annabelle, but did that compensate for a father's absence?

He turned his back on the river and looked on Kew: a scattering of houses in green pastures, with St Anne's spire pointing to heaven, where, if indeed there was a God, his wife would now be, and silently asked for her guidance. Nestling amongst them was his house, his home; but with no Hannah to share it with, he felt a reluctance to return to it and instead slowly walked to her grave. What would she have wanted him to do? As he kneeled, the answer came to him: she would not want him to forsake their child. He was still kneeling by the graveside when Gusta approached from behind with her maidservant and surprised him out of his contemplation.

'Hello, James. Mama told me that your dear wife had died and was buried here. I've come to visit her, James, and bring her flowers.'

'Thank you, Gusta, you are very kind.'

'I hope you won't be leaving us, James, but should you do, may we call on you sometimes? George and I would not want to stop seeing you.'

'Yes, you are both very welcome to visit me, but I won't be stopped from seeing you. You'll come to my concerts with your mother, I hope? Lady Burlington is arranging a soirée for me at Chiswick House and I'm sure you'll be invited to it.'

'Oh, yes. I would much rather go there than into dirty old London. It's a very curious house, isn't it, James, but we like it very much.'

'Yes, but it's really only a villa, Gusta. It was built in the antique Roman style, I'm told. A favoured design of Lord Burlington.'

'He's my godfather, you know, James, and he is Uncle Richard to us.'

'Then I'm sure you'll be invited!'

'What will you be playing?' asked Gusta.

'A selection of preludes and fugues from Bach's *Well-Tempered Clavier.*'

'Well-tempered?' questioned Gusta, laughing. 'How can a keyboard be "well-tempered"?'

'My harpsichord is very well-tempered, I assure you. It never gets cross when I play it,' said James, at which they both laughed.

'I must tell you, James, that I will not be living in England when I'm older,' said Gusta, putting on a sombre look. 'My mother has told me that I am expected to marry my second cousin, the Prince of Brunswick, although she admits that she doesn't really like the House of Brunswick, but she may be prevailed upon. I do wonder what he's like. I have yet to meet him.'

'Well, when you do, I hope you like him and fall in love,' James said affectionally.

There was a very select audience when James gave his recital and few in number due to the small size of the villa, but it did include Princess Augusta and her two eldest children; also his mother-in-law, Elisabeth, who sat herself next to Lord Burlington with his wife on the other side. It was soon evident to James that Elisabeth had Lord Burlington in her sights, when he overheard her recalling her love of his friend William Kent and his devotion to her, with unveiled allusions to their relationship.

James played Bach for the agreed hour before the royal children started fidgeting and Elisabeth coughed several times to indicate that she had heard enough of her son-in-law's playing, after which they gathered in an adjoining room for refreshments and gossip. Elisabeth showed no modesty as she stood by Princess Augusta and Lord Burlington engaged in conversation.

'And how is my Lord Wysop, these days?' she asked sardonically of the princess.

'I really don't know,' said the princess, fanning herself to conceal her embarrassment and turning to look at her two children.

Lord Burlington saw the princess's embarrassment and, with a disapproving look, turned to Elisabeth. 'If you are interested in matters of politics, my dear, I can tell you that Lord Wysop is very active in the House and is tabling a bill on a cider tax but has little support for it. It would hit the working classes too much,' said Burlington.

'Then they might drink less of it,' said Elisabeth scornfully.

'Yes, that is his reason for his bill, but I don't support it. We have our port, let the people have their cider, I say.'

'You are clever, Richard. Put that way, I cannot but agree,' said Elisabeth, smiling beguilingly at him.

Lady Burlington had made little comment throughout the evening, but when James and his mother-in-law were preparing to leave, she confronted Elisabeth. 'Your interest in politics surprises me, my dear, but not your interest in my husband. I advise you that he has never needed a mistress and he doesn't need one now, thank you. Neither would I ever condone it,' she said emphatically. 'Goodnight!'

Elisabeth's mouth dropped in astonishment. 'Well! Goodnight to you, my lady,' was all she could say.

James kept silent until they were in their carriage. 'That was rather embarrassing, Elisabeth, and, if I may say so, spoiled the evening.'

Elisabeth tutted. 'You do not know the communications I've had with Richard or he with me and neither does his wife, so don't make rash conclusions, James. I have known him longer than she has and probably more intimately.'

'What you do in your romantic liaisons is your own affair, but when you are with me, it reflects on me. I don't see you being invited again and probably not myself either.'

'Oh, don't be so prim, James. You really cannot afford to be, with your colour.'

James felt stabbed by the remark but remained silent, immersed in his thoughts. He had goaded her into her recrimination and he knew his mother-in-law held no colour prejudice, and she was right anyway. His colour would always be with him and he was fortunate to have found success despite it. In Kew, he was accepted and befriended by the inhabitants, and being brought up in Chiswick and the only black person apparently in it, he was well recognised throughout the district, but his knowledge of the lives of other negroes haunted him. The thought that he was enjoying a life of privilege which he, a black, had no expectation of, gnawed on his mind, as did what to do with his child, and after some deliberation he decided to visit his friends Dr Lucas and Susie the following day to seek their advice.

10

'Why, if it isn't Smiley!'

The greeting rang through the coffee house as all the heads turned to look at the young black man who carried the name and held his head high. Yes, it was an apt name, some thought. His face wore a wide grin, showing gleaming white teeth which few of the customers could claim to have. His appearance belied his slave origins. His wig was powdered and he was elegantly dressed in a black frock coat with a white cravat and silver buckled shoes.

With open arms, Susie rushed to kiss and embrace him and then turned around to address her customers, all earnest-looking men, until then engaged in discussion or reading newspapers over their cups.

'This is Smiley, my fellow ex-slave whom I sailed across the sea with, all the way from Jamaica,' she announced proudly. 'Eighteen years ago! And look at the gentleman he has become. Gentleman James!'

To the embarrassment of James, some clapping broke out amongst the customers who, by their response and apparent approval, held Susie in esteem.

'Aye, but some of us know him for what he is now: the black musician,' one called out after the clapping.

James's embarrassment was heightened further when Susie's husband, Thomas Lucas, entered the shop from their rooms above. 'Well, I've never heard such clapping in the shop before. Hello, James, welcome back!'

Dr Lucas led James to a table, where three men stood up and shook hands with James and offered him a chair.

'These friends of mine are leading the campaign in the abolitionist movement and you are very welcome to join us, James. In fact, you are very much what we are short of: an ex-slave. Your achievements will add strength to our cause.'

James thoughts went back to his earlier involvement with Thomas's campaigning, which abruptly finished when he was attacked and stoned by a mob on Kennington Common.

Dr Lucas was picking up on James's thoughts. 'Don't be put off by your last experience, James, terrible though it was. That was a hanging crowd. It was a mistake to be there. Our campaigning is now directed more at Parliament and the newspapers.'

One of the friends, who had been reading *The London Chronicle*, lifted his head. 'See this advertisement,' he said, pointing to the paper and reading aloud. '"To be **SOLD**, a **NEGRO** boy about **14 years** old, **warranted free** from any distemper and those fatal to that colour; has been used to **two years** of all kinds of **household work** and to wait on table; his price is £25, and would not be sold but the person he belongs to is leaving off business. Apply at the bar of the **George Coffee House** in **Chancery Lane**, over the gate."'

'Didn't you used to work there?' the man asked of Susie.

'Yes, six years ago. It would be interesting to go there and follow up on the advertisement to find out who is selling him. We know the proprietor very well and I'm sure he would tell us.'

'Yes, we may be able to exert some influence on the owner of the boy to give him his freedom or make it a public cause,' said Thomas. 'At the very least, we could perhaps raise the twenty-five pounds between us to buy him his freedom.'

There were murmurs of assent and some of caution at the suggestion, but it was greeted with immediate approval by Susie and two of the men, and James added his agreement to join them. James felt guilty that he had not continued being active in the fight against slavery and had not used his success in music to benefit the lives of other blacks. Here was a group of white men showing more commitment to the anti-slave cause than he had done.

'Yes, that's an excellent idea, and I would be happy to put up the money myself, but I want to do more,' said James in retrospection. 'Tell me, Thomas, what I can do?'

'Well, for a start, you can use any influence you may have in Princess Augusta's court and any parliamentarians or lords whom you know, anyone who has influence. Make your own experiences more public and join in our protests, James,' said Thomas. 'And come and join us in our debates.'

'And activities. Where the action is,' said one of the three men vehemently. 'Take the protests to the streets.'

'James is not without that experience,' said Thomas pointedly. 'But we are not out to create disturbance but public debate. Keep it lawful and moral. After all, it's the morality of slavery which we question.'

James stood up. 'It's my privilege to be part of your movement, gentlemen,' he said, 'and I will use the colour of my skin and any status I may have on the music platform to promote it further. I pray that I can influence others.'

James was embarrassed by the applause.

'Thank you, James. You are so welcome,' said Susie. 'Now, I think it's best if I go to the George coffee house and find out from Sidney, the owner, who it was that put the advertisement in, and the sooner I go before anyone else makes an offer, the better.'

Susie stopped a chaise outside her premises in Fleet Street and asked the driver to take her to Chancery Lane. As she was carried along the crowded streets, she reflected on how familiar they were to her now and how, like so many of the inhabitants of London, she was drawn to its vitality, its abandon, its crowds, but where a surprise always lay waiting to change perceptions.

'Hello! If it isn't Susie,' cried out Sidney from behind the bar. 'Come back for your job, Susie?'

'No, thank you. I'm happy in my own place, Sidney. Can I speak with you?'

Sidney showed her to a table and sat down with her. He didn't look too happy, thought Susie, and the coffee bar was not as busy as she remembered.

'I've come about the advertisement for a young slave boy. Tell me, Sidney, who's selling him?'

'Don't tell me that you are buying a slave and you, a black! But, you're not the first person to come. I've had two men come already and they were serious enough to pay me a guinea I asked for giving them the information.'

'You haven't changed, have you, Sidney?'

'I haven't, but the bar trade has. It isn't what it was when you were here, Susie. I have to make money, however. They don't come in now for their hands to be read so my takings are not what they were. Are you still reading hands, Susie?'

'No, I don't need to do that at my place. Trade is good enough, but I would be happy to read yours in exchange for the address, Sidney.'

'I asked them for a guinea to see how serious they were, as the friend that's selling the boy doesn't want no time-wasters. It was his idea to use my address and to ask for a guinea but, for you, Susie, I'll give it to you for a reading, but tell me first, why do you of all people want to buy a slave boy?'

'To give him his freedom. Why else? But it is not just me. There's a whole group of supporters campaigning for the end of slavery.'

'Aye, I've heard that is so. Quakers, aren't they? Are you one of them?'

'No, but I'm with them on ending slavery. Now, give me your hand, Sidney, as I must be off.'

Susie looked searchingly at his palm, at his life lines crisscrossing his hard skin. She knew that he had never really got over the death of his wife and thought that she could lift his spirits with her reading.

'I see a woman smiling. She's waiting for you to acknowledge her. She's too shy to speak to you or too proud, but she wants to know you, Sidney. She could be a customer, as I see a cup in the background as well.'

Sidney appeared to reflect and then smiled at a recollection. 'There's a lady who comes in most days and sits alone reading a paper. I see her looking at me sometimes, but I never thought—'

'She's putting a hand out to you. There's a crowd behind her, as well. They could be customers waiting to follow her in. Perhaps that is what you need, Sidney, a wife to help you to run the shop.'

'You are so right, Susie. That is just what I need. Oh! Thank you. I will get into conversation with her next time she's here and get to know her.'

Susie let go of his hand. 'Now, Sidney. Where do I find this slave boy?'

'It's a ship chandler's shop by the river in Wapping. Joshua Green's, it's called. Joshua's getting old and selling up.'

'Thank you, Sidney. Now, I must go.'

'You may've changed my life, Susie, thank you. You've raised my spirits again.'

11

It was a purposeful Dr Lucas who took a barge to Wapping as soon as his wife returned with the information. The humanity of his mission outweighed all the rhetoric he had used against slavery in the past. Now he was giving his argument substance by saving a man from its bonds and it filled him with pride. It may only be one man, and a boy at that, but it was a beginning, and there would be others, he reasoned, perhaps giving substance to a national campaign to free all slaves.

After asking at the quayside, he was directed to the shop and stood looking in, but the interior was so dark he could make nothing out, and he went inside. An old man was sitting on a chair at the back amongst coils of rope, baskets, lamps and tallow candles.

'Joshua Green?' Dr Lucas asked.

'Yes, that be me. What can I do for ye?'

'I've come to buy the slave boy you advertised. Is he here?'

'Then you've come too late, sir, 'ee's bin taken, yesterday.'

'You've sold him? For twenty-five pounds?'

'That's right, and glad he's gone. I'll be shutting the shop down and the missus doesn't want him. Can I sell you any of the stock? We can strike a price.'

'No, thank you, I'm only interested in the boy. Where has he gone to? Who's bought him?'

'A wig maker in the Hay Market took him. Wanted him for his stables, he said.'

'Do you know his name?'

'He did say, but I don't remember proper. Could have been Cotton or such like.'

Dr Lucas thanked the chandler and took a chaise to the Hay Market to look for a wig maker of that name. The only one he could find there was named Sutton, but the similarity of the name prompted him to make enquiries on the premises.

'Did you buy a slave boy yesterday, from Joshua Green in Wapping?' he asked of the man behind the counter. The man frowned as Dr Lucas waited for him to reply.

'Why do you ask, sir? What I do is my business. I make and sell wigs, sir.'

'I'm sure you do, and very good wigs, I hear, but I'm enquiring about a slave boy bought for twenty-five pounds from Joshua Green. Do you have him, sir?'

'As I said, sir, why do you ask?'

'I would wish to make an offer for him and for you to make a profit by selling him to me. Is he here?'

'Yes, just about. A very disgruntled young man. Put him on cleaning out the stables straight away. Why do you want him? What's your offer?'

'I'll give you thirty pounds for him. That will more than reimburse you for your troubles.'

'Thirty pounds? Now, sir, why should a gentleman like you be wanting him so much?'

Dr Lucas decided to resort to deceit, reasoning that the ends justified it. 'I'm a doctor and I have reason to believe that the boy has got distemper, which, as you may know, is very contagious, and he should not be mixing with other people.'

The wig maker looked visibly agitated and distraught at the

news. 'Well, I'll thank thee for taking him off my hands then and I'll take the thirty pounds for my troubles. I'll get him and his bag for ye if you wait awhile.'

Five minutes later he reappeared holding a walking stick, prodding a confused-looking, curly-haired, coal-black young man, wearing a ragged smock and carrying a sailor's canvas bag.

'Here he be. A strong youth, as ye can see. I hope you have work enough for his keep. I thank thee for taking him, Doctor, and may the good Lord bless you for your good works,' the wig maker said, grasping the proffered thirty-pound notes off the doctor. 'And when you need another wig, sir, I hope you remember me.'

Dr Lucas told the boy to follow him as he made for the river to catch a barge to Temple Pier.

'What's your name, boy?' he asked on the way.

'Benjamin, sir.'

'So, it'll be Ben I'll call you, and do you know how old you are, Ben?'

'Fifteen, I think I am, sir.'

'Well, Ben, to put your mind at ease, I'll tell you now that we're going to my coffee house, where you'll meet my wife and child and where you'll stay until we decide what's best for you. By the way, my name is Dr Thomas Lucas.'

Ben's jaw dropped and, although he had many questions to ask of this stranger who had claimed him, he retained a silence which he had long practised in the presence of white people.

It was night-time when they arrived at the home of his new owner, where Ben was amazed to find that Dr Lucas's wife was also black. She welcomed him as a friend and invited him to eat at their kitchen table after he had washed in the scullery.

'When you've eaten, I'll show you where you'll be sleeping until it's been decided what you'll be doing,' Susie said. 'That can wait until tomorrow, when everything will be discussed and then we'll get you some better clothes.'

That night, as Benjamin lay on the floor of the shop, wrapped a blanket around himself and put his head on his canvas bag, he wondered if it was all a dream and, if so, would he wake up tomorrow back in the stables?

Next morning, James, Susie and Dr Lucas, and his three friends, met in the coffee house to discuss the boy's future, and Dr Lucas told Ben to sit with them.

'You must be wondering why I have brought you here, Ben. These gentlemen and I have bought you your freedom. We are giving it to you now. You are no longer a slave to anyone,' Dr Lucas announced solemnly. 'You are a free man, Ben, at liberty to do whatever you wish. Whatever you do now is your own decision.'

Ben was stunned into silence as he contemplated the significance of what he had heard. He had only ever done what had been expected of him or what he had been told to do. What was he to do with this freedom, he asked himself? Go back to Jamaica where he came from? He would like to do that, he reflected, but he knew of no blacks there who were free, and would he keep his freedom if he went?

'Until you decide what you want to do, my wife and I have agreed that you can stay here and help in the coffee shop,' said Dr Lucas, 'and we'll pay you a weekly wage. It will give you time to get used to your new circumstances and we'll be here to help you.'

The offer was met with universal approval by the small group and, in turn, they shook hands with a dumbfounded Ben and congratulated him.

'I've been in your situation, Ben, and I know how you must be feeling,' said James. 'You can't believe it, can you? I will help you all I can to get used to freedom.'

Dr Lucas turned to the men, aware of other customers listening, some behind their newspapers.

'You know that I have been campaigning against slavery since my return from Jamaica eighteen years ago but, in all that time, we've made no real headway. This is just a small step. A drop in the ocean, but it can cause ripples if we publicise it. I know that we are all aware of the opposition we will face, but it is for us to raise the argument against slavery to new levels. I propose that we call ourselves "The Abolitionists" and ask as many men of title and rank as we know to sign a petition for the abolition of slavery and announce it in the newspapers and journals. We could start a national fund to buy out other slaves and advertise our aims. We could hold public meetings and make representation to the church and to Parliament and even to the king to end slavery in this so-called Christian country.'

'Would not just baptising them all make them Christians and give them their freedom?' asked one of the men.

James asked to reply to the question. 'No, I know that the solicitor-general, Sir Philip Yorke, pronounced on that only recently. It is a commonly held fallacy, but it wasn't held up in court.'

James reflected that it was only because of Annabelle's persistent pleading with her father that he had been given his freedom. He knew that there was fierce opposition to ending slavery and that it was deep-rooted in the country, with many more adherents than opponents ready to fight to the last slave to keep it.

'I agree with all that Dr Lucas suggests and henceforth I will devote myself to its abolition,' declared James. 'Let us join together to put an end to this morally unjustifiable practice.'

'Well, with your colour it will be like geese asking for the abolition of Christmas,' interjected a customer.

'Then all the more reason for you to join in,' responded Dr Lucas.

'No, I come for my coffee, not to put the country's economy in jeopardy,' came back the reply amidst a general hubbub as others shouted to be heard.

'Gentlemen! Gentlemen!' called Dr Lucas for quiet. 'We are

open for coffee, of course, but if you wish to join in the debate against slavery, or even if you are in favour of it, please come on Monday nights at seven-thirty. Either way, you will all be very welcome.'

12

It was a cold, wintery scene with light snow falling as James made his morning journey by river from his house in Kew to London, and his mood reflected it. There would be few more visits he would be making to the royal children. He would miss their banter, their familiarity and their earnestness to please him. He had occupied a privileged position in their lives, one that could not be sustained against the animosity of Lord Wysop. Alighting at Savoy Wharf, amongst the labyrinth of tenemented streets and alleys, he was immediately accosted by a street prostitute with a nosegay of violets pinned to her breast.

'Are you free, sir? I 'ave a warm place. Only a shilling to you, sir.'

'No, thank you,' he said, trying not to engage her eyes. He knew, if he did, she would take it as an interest in her offer.

'I never 'ad a black man 'afore,' she retorted, almost pleading as she stretched out her arm.

He felt repelled as he avoided her touch and looked ahead for a carriage to take him to Savile House, where the princess and her children were now in winter residence, but his attention was drawn to the newspaper seller, whose placard caught his eye.

"**Sudden Death of Lord Burlington**"

He handed over his two pence and fervently read the lead article on the front page. Lord Burlington had been found dead in bed at Chiswick House the previous day by his wife, Lady Burlington, née Lady Dorothy Savile, he read. The cause of death was unknown and a post-mortem would be made. He was age thirty-eight and was not known to be suffering from any illness. Lady Dorothy was recovering from the shock in the care of her daughter, Charlotte Cavendish, Marchioness of Hartington.

As James read the news, he felt the grievous loss of a friend, patron and benefactor, suddenly no more, and his thoughts went to the scene in Chiswick House and the distress that must be pervading there. Lord Burlington had lived for his art and his architecture, and would be remembered for them, but now, it was his wife and daughters who must be remembered. He recalled the recent recital he had given at Chiswick House and the animosity shown between his own mother-in-law and Lady Burlington. Had Elisabeth really been in a relationship with the lord, as she had insinuated, and how would she feel now? He decided to delay going to Savile House and instead to call on Elisabeth to inform her of the death.

On his arrival, Elisabeth opened the door only slightly, looking embarrassed and dishevelled as though she had just got out of bed.

'Oh, it's you, James. I wasn't expecting you. You should have told me,' she said, keeping the door ajar. 'I have company.'

James hesitated, aware of his unwelcome intrusion. 'I'm sorry to have disturbed you, Elisabeth, but I have sad news. Lord Burlington has died.'

'Oh, my God!' she cried out. 'Burly? Died? How?'

A muffled cough came from the interior as Elisabeth held the door.

'He was found dead in bed by his wife. A terrible shock for her.'

'A shock for me, too, I tell you. I need time for it to sink in. Oh, dear! Leave me to my grief, James. I have much to think of.'

James took his leave with his suspicions of his mother-in-law's amorous liaisons surfacing in his mind again, but he felt no satisfaction in the knowledge. With snow still falling, he took a sedan chair to Savile House. On opening the door, the servant confided in him that Lord Wysop was with the princess but that Prince George was expecting him.

It was Gusta who welcomed him as he entered the music room. 'James, I fear that you may be leaving us,' she said tearfully. 'Mama has said so.'

'That is up to your mother, my dear, but I hope that reason will prevail and that I may yet continue your tuition.'

'But I don't think so, James. Not according to George.'

George and Edward entered the room.

'Did I hear my name mentioned?' George asked, looking intently at Gusta.

'Yes. Are you surprised?' questioned Gusta defiantly.

'No. I expect you've been blackening it.'

'No, George,' James hastened to add. 'Gusta was giving me her opinion, that I may not be your tutor for much longer.'

'That may be true, but I have you know that I have spoken in your favour to Mama and Lord Wysop, though I cannot disagree with their argument that a change of tutor would give us a different perspective on music.'

'It's old Wysop who dictates to you,' intervened Edward, 'and Mama agrees with everything he says and you do everything he tells you to do.'

'Lord Wysop only has our interest at heart,' asserted George.

'Then why don't we have another tutor as well as keeping James?' asked Edward.

'Mama is bedevilled already at the cost of our education,' said George. 'You do not know the problems Father left to her. She says we must live within our means.'

'Grandpa pays for everything, doesn't he?' asked Edward. 'He's the king. He can do anything.'

'Grandpa gives us all an allowance and Mama says we must learn to live within it. People go to prison if they get into debt,' said George.

'Would we go to prison?' asked Gusta.

'No, Grandpa wouldn't allow that,' said George.

James tapped the table for attention. 'Well, now that I am here, I suggest that we get on with our music for today. I thought that I could introduce you to more of the music of Scarlatti.'

The three children gave audible sighs, showing that they would much prefer to continue their argument, but James resolutely started his instruction. Later that morning a servant came in and told James that Princess Augusta would like to see him in her apartment before he left. When he was shown in, he was not surprised to see Lord Wysop sitting beside her.

The princess turned to him benignly. 'James, I wish to thank you for your diligent instruction of my children. I know that you are very fond of them and they of you, but now that they are older, we think it would be of benefit to them to have a change of tutor. Lord Wysop has been making enquires and has found one.'

Lord Wysop nodded in agreement. 'Yes, a sensible, knowledgeable and well-bred man,' he said emphatically, looking at James disapprovingly.

The princess continued to smile at James kindly. 'I do appreciate all the instruction you have given the children and I'm sure they will continue to benefit from it. I look forward to seeing you again, James, but thank you for now,' she said with the inference that their interview was over.

Lord Wysop followed James to the door and then, stiffening up his body and assuming an air of superiority, addressed him. 'George spoke strongly in your favour, so much so that it confirmed to me that your influence on him was unacceptable. He will have his music instruction by a professional teacher in future and will be able to evaluate it unemotionally. Goodbye… and speak to the keeper of the purse if you need to claim for your services,' he said with a look of disdain.

James left Savile House feeling sad and humiliated, regretting that he had not said his final goodbye to the children. He wondered if the princess and Lord Wysop knew of the death of Lord Burlington.

It was dusk and the snow was still falling, melting into the slush and water of the streets, as he hailed a chairman to take him back to the Savoy Stairs. The bearer, a strong Irish fellow, swore to himself as he ran along, cursing the potholes and puddles as he tried to avoid them. When James paid the man off, the same prostitute who had approached him that morning sidled up to him, smiling beguilingly.

'Hello, sir, are you free now, sir? I 'ave a warm place to go to, not far away. A little loving, perhaps, sir?'

James pondered for seconds. Yes, that was what he was missing, "a little loving". He had never felt the need for a street woman and had remained faithful to his wife's memory. The young woman's pleading felt inviting and, for a moment, stirred his emotions, but the memory of his wife was still strong within him.

'Oh, how I miss you, Hannah!' he almost cried out in grief, before walking away.

13

James returned home to find his housekeeper in tears and scarcely able to speak.

'We've been burgled, sir,' she said, between sobs. 'I went out in the morning for some provisions, sir, and when I came back the door was open. Someone must have a key, as there's no sign of entry, but some things have gone, sir, and they've been upstairs.'

'You mean you left the house unattended with the door open?' he asked harshly. 'Where was Matthew?'

'He went to Chiswick House, sir, with the condolence letter you gave him to take. He probably stopped at the Punch Tavern on his way back, as it is his custom. I was back by midday, sir.'

'You are not disparaging another servant, are you, because of your own negligence, surely?' James felt his anger rise. 'You left the house unattended and the door unlocked, didn't you?'

The housekeeper only cried the more, and as no answer was forthcoming, James assumed the crying was a cover for her carelessness.

'So, what has gone then, that you know of?' James asked, still in a tone of rebuke.

The housekeeper's crying intensified.

'Take control of yourself and tell me,' demanded James.

The housekeeper dabbed her eyes and looked pityingly at James. 'The silver has been taken and the clock has gone, sir, and I think some things have been taken from your bedroom, as it's all disturbed, sir,' she said between tears.

In a sudden alarm, James ran upstairs to his bedroom to find his cupboards had been broken into and the contents strewn on the floor. He looked under his bed, the place where he had always kept the treasured bequest from Patch. The place where Patch had always kept it, but the box was not there. The doubloons had gone, stolen! Of the fifty doubloons Patch left to him he had only spent twenty, and with the loss of the remaining thirty the last of his inheritance from Patch had gone. He went cold at the thought and damned himself for his own carelessness for not keeping them in a safer place. It was only out of sentiment for Patch that he had kept the doubloons under the bed.

He confronted his trembling housekeeper again but received only more tears and distraught apologies. He searched the house, hoping to find a clue, any clue that might lead him to his loss, but as he searched so did his despair increase. The doubloons had been a surety for his future. Now that his tutorage at the Court had been terminated, there was only what remained of Hannah's dowry. He slumped into his chair as the precariousness of his situation hit him. Any income from his piano recitals was little and unsure. Money owed to him by Princess Augusta was unlikely to be paid. He had lived comfortably on his meagre income by supplementing it from his wife's dowry and his doubloons. Now he knew he would have to live more frugally. He aroused himself from his introspection and called his housekeeper.

'This puts your employment here in jeopardy, I might tell you,' he said in anger. 'Not just because of your carelessness but also whether I can now afford to keep you. Did you see anything untoward when you came back?'

The housekeeper hesitated, trembling even more. 'There was a note left on the bed, sir.'

'A note? Why didn't you say so? Have you got it?'

The housekeeper pulled out a crumbled piece of paper from her apron pocket and, saying she was sorry, nervously handed it to James.

James read out the three scrawled words. 'Thank you, nigger.'

A shiver went through James's body as he repeated the word he had last heard on board the ship which had brought him here. It had been uttered by the vilest of the crew, Masters, who had been given the lash for his attempted rape of Susie.

No sooner had he spoken and his housekeeper had resumed her crying than there was a knock on the door which he went to answer. Standing in the doorway was Francis, looking anxious and holding James's own son, Henry, in his arms.

'I have bad news, James,' said Francis. 'Annabelle has a fever. It came over her yesterday and she is much worse today, so I've brought the baby. She thinks it may be better if he stays with you until she recovers.'

James was taken aback. Now, his indecision about his child had been settled for him, if only temporarily.

'I'm sorry, Francis. Of course, I'll have the baby. I can get a nurse for him. In the meantime my housekeeper can help me to look after him.'

'Annabelle thinks it's better for him to be here so that he doesn't catch her fever and insisted that I brought him to you immediately. She's not well enough to come herself.'

'I'm sorry. What can it be? Are you alright?'

'Yes, I'm alright, but I'm worried about Annabelle. She has the fever badly.'

'Have you called a doctor?' asked James.

'No, but I will do so tomorrow if she's no better. I've got a bundle of the baby's clothes to leave, but there's his cot and other things which you may want to collect later.'

'Yes, thank you, Francis, but I will get what I need locally. If it's a fever, it's better if I stay away until it's passed, if only for the baby's sake.'

James called out for his housekeeper, who had retreated to the kitchen. 'You can make amends now for your carelessness by helping me to look after the baby until I get a nurse for him.'

'Oh, yes, I'll take him and look after him. I've had enough experience with my own.'

'It will only be for a short time while Annabelle recovers,' he said, handing the baby to her.

Two days later, James received a letter from Francis informing him that Annabelle had developed blistering all over her body. The doctor had diagnosed smallpox and feared that she may not live long. It was inadvisable to visit her now, but she sent James her never-ending love and asked him to give his child all the love and kindness which she had so much hoped to give him. James anxiously examined the baby for signs of the disease and, fearing contagion, he continued to do so, but with profound relief he found none.

Seven days later Francis came again in a very distressed state and, in between sobs, said that Annabelle had died. Both men held on to each other, unable to control their tears.

'Is the baby alright?' asked Francis finally.

'Yes, he's fine, thank God, and you? Are you alright?' asked James.

'Yes. The doctor asked me if I had chickenpox when I was a child and I remembered I had. He suggested that could be the reason that I had escaped smallpox, but it's only his theory.'

James questioned that as he had never had chickenpox, was he at greater risk?

'But how do you think Annabelle caught it?'

Tears welled from Francis's eyes. 'An itinerant she took pity on. An old woman she let stay in the outhouse while she found work in the village and Annabelle fed her. She had it. It was only three days before she broke out in a fever, but she left and we never saw her again. She was found dead in a ditch the next week, covered with the pox. Annabelle said she thought the woman knew she might have had it and left so as not to endanger us.'

'She had such high opinions of everyone and was so caring. She was a mother and sister to me in my childhood,' said James. 'She did so much for me. How sad that she will not see Henry grow up.'

'Yes, Henry was the child we never had. He brought her happiness for a short time. I don't know how I'll manage without her. I may go back to the sea again. I couldn't continue living in the house without her.'

'Give yourself time, Francis. Don't make rash decisions while you are so distressed,' advised James.

When Francis departed, James felt his own resilience drain away. Bereft of love, of the people who had meant so much to him, his life suddenly felt empty, and he sank into a mood of depression, heavy with the thought of another burial ahead of him. When, two days later, he watched Annabelle's coffin being lowered into the ground, he was overwhelmed with tears.

Susie saw his distress and turned to him, holding him close. 'Give way to your grief, James; don't bottle it up. Let it out, but don't drown in self-pity. Remember Hannah left you someone to live for: your own son. He needs you now more than ever.'

Dr Lucas put his arm over James's shoulder. 'Yes, your son is your first priority, James, but don't forget you have our black cause to care about as well.'

James knew they were trying to alleviate his suffering by being mindful of the future. Annabelle's sister, Felicity, and her husband, George, joined them and added their reassurances.

'Remember, we will be here for you, James, and for the baby, whenever you need help,' said Felicity kindly. 'Francis has offered us Jamaica House when he goes back to sea. Imagine us living in Chiswick again, in Father's old house,' she added almost joyfully.

George looked at his wife reprehensibly. 'Felicity, this is not the time to be rejoicing.'

'I didn't mean to sound that I was, but if Annabelle was here, then I know that she would be happy for us.'

'If Annabelle was here, then we wouldn't be having her house, would we?' said George.

Felicity cast her eyes down at the reproach. 'Annabelle would understand me. She always did.'

Next day, James resolved to make enquires for a nursemaid for the baby at a London employment agency which led to a number of young women being recommended, amongst which, with the help of his housekeeper, he chose one whose manner and age was more in the accord of Hannah's.

14

Dr Lucas's reminder to James not to forget the black cause surfaced in James's mind as he watched Ben happily at work in the garden. He had done little to relieve other slaves of their servitude. Giving just one his freedom jarred on his conscience and he resolved to take up the cause again, and on the following Monday evening he went to Susie's coffee shop to join in Dr Lucas's anti-slavery meeting, where he was called upon to speak. He recounted his own experience, not omitting his good fortune and privileged lifestyle despite his colour. Some members of his audience questioned his commitment to the cause, claiming that anyone who had escaped servitude was exceptional and failed to put slavery in the pillory where it belonged.

'It was a travesty,' shouted out one. 'You are almost a justification for it!'

'Far be it for me to justify slavery any more than I could justify the monarchy. I was only saved from slavery by my benefactor, the good Captain Cudlip. Saving one slave does not help the thousands who are still tied and bound to it.'

'It benefits our country's economy,' cried another. 'You wouldn't be drinking coffee without it either. Who do you think would work on the coffee plantations otherwise?'

'That doesn't justify slavery, and nothing can. If you look at it objectively, it serves to keep workers' wages low and deprives human beings of their inalienable rights,' said Dr Lucas.

'We would be worse off without it, and most slaves are heathens, anyway,' claimed another.

The audience disassembled into fractious groups arguing amongst themselves and, with a shake of his head in forbearance, Dr Lucas invited James to join him and Susie upstairs for a meal.

The following day, James was surprised when a newspaper report was brought to his attention, criticising him, an ex-slave, for associating the monarchy with the anti-slave movement. However, James was not the only person to have it brought to his attention. So had Lord Wysop, who lost no time in conveying it to George, now heir apparent, as an act of disloyalty. At the suggestion from Lord Wysop, George requested James to call on him, and when he did so, he found that Lord Wysop was also present.

'James,' began George, somewhat apprehensively, 'Lord Wysop tells me that you have been publicly expressing disloyalty to the crown and that you cannot justify having a monarchy. Is this true, James?'

'Not disloyalty, sir, just questioning the justification for it. It was an anti-slavery meeting.'

'James, I know full well your slave background. You have spoken of it many times to myself and you have every right to campaign against it, but I think you are wrong to bring me into it. I may not be king yet, but I am king-in-waiting and would expect loyalty to the throne, particularly from my friends. What do you say to that, James?'

'I respect your sovereignty, sir, and would never speak against it. The country will be fortunate indeed to have you on the throne and you have, as you so rightly deserve, my full loyalty.'

'May I say something, sir?' interjected Lord Wysop.

'Of course. I will hear you out, Lord Wysop, but I'm sure that James speaks as a friend,' said the prince.

'I trust that is as I speak, too, as a friend, but I also speak as a guardian to you and advisor to you and to your mother, George,' said Lord Wysop. 'I say that James is taking advantage of your friendship towards him and has dragged you, the heir and crown prince, into public debate of justifying your own position, and the monarchy. Not only that but he has also had the temerity to embroil you in the slavery debate,' and turning to James, he said, 'You, young sir, have used your position and the privilege of your friendship of Prince George to further your own ends.'

'I'm sure that James bears me no ill-will and has every reason to speak out against slavery, having been born of one himself, but he does not speak for me,' countered George.

'I can only speak from my own experience and observation,' said James.

'But do you not recognise the benefit it brings to the empire, James? Who would populate the Americas without it? Who would grow the coffee and the cotton there?' asked George.

'George is right. It is evident that you have no loyalty to the throne nor to the country,' said Lord Wysop to James. 'You have taken advantage of George's friendship towards you and have shown that you are unfit to be his tutor,' and, turning to George, he said, 'I will speak to your mother and I'm sure she will take my counsel on your behalf.'

Lord Wysop saw James as an irritant in his relationship with the prince, as well as a constant reminder of his past infidelity with James's mother-in-law, Elisabeth, which, if it was again made public, could not only invalidate his political ambitions for high office but also lose George's mother affection for him.

'My mother looks to me for counsel as well. I may be young, but I am not without knowledge and understanding of people's behaviour or motives,' replied George with strong overtones. 'Remember, Lord Wysop, I have been brought up in court circles and am not unaware of the intrigues and schemes that have been plotted in them. My mother is not without knowledge of them, either, and has never ceased to warn me and protect me from them.'

'Then you will know, Your Highness, if I can be so immodest as to claim some accountability for her knowledge, that I am entirely in accord with your mother,' replied Lord Wysop. 'And we share concern for your association with an ex-slave. It will not look good when you are king, and the American colonies look to you for their interests. It is not in their interests to free slaves. Not good at all. Not for them and consequently not for our country.'

'I do not see James as an ex-slave,' said George forcefully. 'He is a most accomplished musician and recognised as such. He was also a very good friend of my father's, as you well know, and, if for no other reason, will continue to be a friend of mine.'

Lord Wysop took his leave, feeling embittered at having lost the argument but knowing that he could not gainsay the prince. It was not only George's association with an ex-slave that discomforted him but, as a strong loyalist to the institution of the crown, that it should not become entangled into the increasingly febrile slave argument. He never felt at ease in James's presence, knowing how much James knew of his previous dalliances with James's mother-in-law, Elisabeth, putting James in a position to expose him to the princess through George or even to publicly expose him and spoil his political ambitions, wilfully or otherwise.

Meanwhile, Lord Wysop was far from James's mind, which was preoccupied with his own financial status. He had lived on his legacy from Patch and had now spent it. His two main benefactors, Lord Burlington and Prince Frederick, had died. His earnings from his concerts were meagre, with some of them performed for charity and others at the request of nobles holding out promise of payment, most of which were never honoured. He had his household and housekeeper to maintain and his child's nursemaid to pay, as well as their keep. Payment due to him for his tuition of George had long been promised but had never materialised. He knew that Princess Augusta was dependant on the king for financial support and that royal patronage was considered payment enough. Nevertheless, he decided that he would pursue his claim through George and, with this in mind, brought it up at their next meeting.

George sighed when he did so. 'Mama never has money enough to spare and she says she has to be frugal with it. She doesn't like asking the king for more than she gets, but I will ask her for you, James.'

James held out little hope of payment materialising, knowing that no decision would be made by the princess without the unlikely approval of Lord Wysop. He resolved to increase his public piano concerts and, with this in mind, wrote to his benefactor, Lady Burlington, whom he had not seen since the death of her husband, asking if he could call on her at Chiswick House. Her immediate invitation lifted his spirits, and when he arrived, he was warmly greeted.

'James, how good to see you. You must update me on your engagements. Since my husband died, I've been out of touch with everyone. How are you doing, pray?'

'I've had few engagements in recent months,' James began.

'Then I must take up the torch again, James, and shine some light onto you,' she responded. 'Instead of just being your benefactor, I declare myself patron, too, and will announce my return to society at the same time. My mourning period is over and, although Richard will never be forgotten, I am ready to open my doors to society again.'

'I do thank you, my lady, for your kindness and support.'

'You are unique, James, in the musical world. Not only your colour and origins which distinguish you but in your playing as well, and I declare that as your patron, I will endeavour to tell the world.'

James felt overwhelmed by Lady Dorothy's enthusiasm and could only thank her profusely, at which she raised her hands to refrain him. 'One thing I can arrange immediately is another recital here, and I will invite friends who may give you more engagements. You would be surprised at whom I have on my lists, James.'

Lady Burlington lived up to her word and, as well as another recital at Burlington House, he received invitations from impresarios for further engagements.

15

George looked earnestly at James, hesitating before speaking.

'There is something else, something very personal, I must talk to someone about, and I speak to you in confidence as a friend who has known me for a long time. I have been introduced to the sister of the Duke of Cumberland, Lady Sarah Lennox, and like her very much. I have feelings for her, but I don't think she feels the same way for me. She is only fifteen and probably doesn't know what love is. I am twenty-one now, James, but have met very few ladies. The king called for me and my mother to visit him and told me that he was surprised that I had not yet married. He is very ill and concerned about the succession. He suggested that Princess Caroline of Brunswick would be an appropriate choice and beneficial to the country, but I told him that she does not appeal to me. My mother did not think she was suitable either. She thinks I am not yet ready for marriage and should not be rushed into it.'

'She has probably taken advice from Lord Wysop again, but she may be right, George,' advised James.

'Then I will put it to Lord Wysop myself. He has my interest at heart, he keeps telling me. I am born for the happiness or misery of a great nation and consequently must often act contrary to my passion.'

It was a month later when George was called upon to see the king again and when he did so with his mother, he saw a great deterioration in him. He was falling in and out of consciousness and unable to talk coherently, and it was of little surprise to George when it was reported the following day that the king had died.

Unknown to George, Lord Wysop had already been searching the credentials of European dynasties for a suitable marriage for George in anticipation of his succession to the throne. In October 1760 George succeeded to the throne as George III and Lord Wysop's search for a suitable marriage throughout the European dynasties intensified. His preference for the wife-to-be coincided with George's own preference, a foreign princess, preferably German Protestant, centred on disposition and child-bearing possibilities. Eventually, the bride chosen by Lord Wysop was Princess Charlotte of Mecklenburge-Strelitz, who was age seventeen with nine siblings, and described by one contemporary as "small and crooked with a true mulatto face". It was not until the following year that a marital agreement was reached on the advice of the king's ministers. George somewhat reluctantly agreed to the choice, although he did not meet her until the day of their wedding, only a day after she had arrived. They were married the same evening at St James's Church at the Chapel Royal, but such a speedy marriage was not unconventional in royal circles.

At the announcement, the population of the country, and particularly the citizens of London, celebrated the royal wedding and the heralding of an approaching coronation in Westminster Abbey as if in a fever and people could talk of nothing else. Both were celebrated with special brews of beer and large-scale provision of food and drink to the poor for them to drink to George's health. "Young George" was also popular with the people for, as Prince of Wales, he represented probity and favoured peace terms to end to the war with France, arguing that continuation of it would risk national bankruptcy.

Despite his long-term relationship with George, James was

not expecting an invitation to the coronation so was surprised to receive one. At the ceremony in Westminster Abbey he found himself amongst the country's dignitaries and courtiers, but the ceremony did not live up to the occasion due to poor organisation, not least because the groom of the stole, ended up carrying the lord mayor's sword instead of the sword of state which had been mislaid. The banquet was also chaotic, with no places reserved for some of the leading aristocrats, while the champion's horse backed into George, instead of away from him. Nevertheless, George maintained his composure, looking serious and dignified, and after the banquet walked amongst his guests, chatting amiably to them before he noticed James and immediately approached him.

Many of the guests had looked askance at James and were surprised to see the king engage him in conversation.

'I personally think you could make a significant contribution to the colonies in the Americas, James, as my ambassador. We may not then lose so many,' George said facetiously. 'But, needless to say, it would cause too much outrage from the settlers there. I put it to Lord Wysop and he said it could even start a rebellion. Imagine, James, did you ever think that you could be the cause of a rebellion?'

'I don't take your suggestion seriously and I hope Lord Wysop didn't either,' responded James. 'My relationship with him is difficult enough. Ha, here he comes!'

Lord Wysop was approaching towards, them looking angry and agitated, before he turned to George. 'May I speak to you confidentially?' he asked, putting himself between George and James. 'If I may give you my advice, Your Majesty, you may find your other guests are expecting your pleasure and are more worthy of it. Indeed, they must find it strange that you can find common ground with a freed black slave.'

'Then you must tell them, Lord Wysop. You surprise me. You have known me as long as you have known James and therefore must know that our friendship goes back to my childhood. It should be a cause of celebration, not condemnation.'

'Not to our colonists in the Americas, Your Majesty,' replied the lord. 'They run their plantations on slave labour and do not share your beneficence towards freed slaves.'

'Slaves or not, they will all look to me as their king and to dispense justice and, although I may be young and new to kingship, I intend to act according to my conscience,' said George.

Lord Wysop gave James a withering look. His presence always infuriated him, not only for bringing back memories of Elisabeth, whom he would rather forget, but also because of his friendship with George and James's rise in society against its accepted norms.

'All the more reason to be aware of those who will take advantage of your friendship to promote their own interests, Your Majesty,' Lord Wysop said, glowering at James.

'My father had a long friendship with James and, if that was the only reason for me to continue with it, that would be sufficient. Being king does not change it, Lord Wysop, but more than that, my friendship with James goes back to my childhood, as you know, and I hold James in esteem for what he has accomplished despite his origins, whatever they may be. I have you know I like James, always have and always will.'

Lord Wysop looked ever angrier as he turned his back on James. 'That may be so, but as your advisor it is my responsibility to warn you of the possible repercussions of you continuing your friendship with him. It is not only his colour and background; he is not a man of substance either.'

James faced up to Lord Wysop and spoke with dignity. 'My colour is what it is and I do not have to apologise for it. I am bereft of the benefits of birth that you have been given, but I am proud of my achievements, Lord Wysop. I think that your objection to me is more than dislike but of fear. Fear of the knowledge I have of you, but you need not worry, my lord, for I will not use it against you.'

Lord Wysop suffered a blood rush and his face coloured. 'Fear?

Fear of you? I have never heard such impertinence. A veiled threat, if I ever heard one. Furthermore, I was addressing the king, not you, sir, and wish to continue to do so in privacy. May I, Your Majesty?'

George raised his hands to calm the anger. 'Yes, of course. Do please excuse me, James,' said George benignly.

When the door closed behind James, Lord Wysop addressed George. 'You see now how this man, this ex-slave, uses your friendship to serve his own ends? It is my duty to tell you, as your advisor, to rid yourself of him. Whatever he meant to you in the past, is in the past. Questions are already being asked amongst the Lords as to whether my position as your advisor is being usurped by an ex-slave, would you believe it? It will not be long before questions are openly raised in Parliament and your friendship will be exposed to the world.'

'Exposed? It is nothing that I am ashamed of,' said George.

'But you will be held up to ridicule. Can you not imagine what the news-sheets will make of it? You are king now, George, and must act accordingly.'

16

'Have you thought of re-marrying, James?'

The question came from Lady Burlington as she was sitting with James after giving one of his recitals she had arranged at Chiswick House.

'No. I don't think anyone could take the place of Hannah,' he responded soulfully.

'But you are young, James. Too young to close the door on the possibility. You still have your life ahead of you.'

James reflected on the possibility. His earnings were erratic. He had a child to look after and was still in love with his deceased wife, if only in memory. No, he had not thought of re-marrying.

Lady Burlington had good reason to ask the question, as she had invited several unattached young ladies to the concert, but she was also concerned for James, that he was still mourning the death of his wife. As a widow herself, she knew of the need to face up to the world after suffering a bereavement and hopefully to fill the emptiness with another meaningful relationship; although she herself had not yet found such a person, she had not given up hope.

'Come, James, we must talk to our guests. Let us amble round. I know there are many here who wish to meet you.'

Although James suspected the intensions of Lady Burlington, he knew they were well meant and amiably agreed to be escorted around and introduced to her guests. He was well aware that his colour attracted interest from some people, many of whom had no opportunity, if indeed they had any interest, of ever meeting anyone of colour, let alone one born a slave. Rarely was it the case for his colour, far be it for his slave roots, to be actually mentioned in conversation. No, rather it was inferred in the constantly expressed surprise that he, an outsider of African origins, knew anything of Brahms or Beethoven or could even play a piano. The more he mixed in society, the more he became aware of the prejudice which existed in it, but he was comforted by the thought that his hostess seemed oblivious to it. If Lady Burlington was expecting an introduction to lead to James establishing a relationship with an admirer, she was to be disappointed. The reactions to introductions usually followed a pattern. After the usual expressions of delight at his exoticism and surprise of his musical ability came the anticipated questions of his antecedents. Was he really an African? How did he come to England? Where did he learn to play? It was apparent to James that few, if any, of the guests had ever met a black person or even seen one, let alone spoken to one, but he met his inquisitors politely and with patient tolerance.

Reflecting on the repeated questioning he met with, his mind turned again to his roots. Was his father really the massa whom he vaguely remembered? The white man holding a whip and threatening to use it on him? The man who had sold him to the highest bidder? Was it possible that man could have any love for his child? His thoughts went back to his mother. Had she felt a wrench at his being taken away from her? Could she have loved him? He remembered her telling him to be strong and not to show any weakness, but she had not spoken of any love for him.

On his return home, feeling despondent and alone, he was

surprised to find a note from Felicity asking him to visit her and he would get a surprise. In anticipation he immediately set off for Jamaica House to visit her and on arrival was indeed surprised to find Francis, who had returned home from his voyaging overseas. Francis was desirous of putting his sailing days behind him and establishing himself on land again although feeling bereft of his late wife, Annabelle. He said he was looking for new interests to help him to settle down, so James suggested that he started by coming to his next concert which Lady Burlington had already arranged at Chiswick House.

Francis readily agreed and when James introduced Francis to Lady Burlington before his recital, James was surprised to see her reaction. As Francis kissed her proffered hand, she blushed and her body gave a slight tremble.

'Francis has just returned from an overseas voyage,' James said.

'Oh, I would love to hear about it,' she said to Francis. 'Do come and sit down and tell me about it. I've never ventured abroad. Please excuse me, James,' she said, leading Francis to the chairs.

After giving his recital, James was surprised to see that that they immediately resumed their conversation and appeared engrossed in each other.

Later, Francis came up to him and thanked him for introducing her. 'She has a very wide outlook on life; for someone who has never been abroad, she has a very wide knowledge. I find her very interesting,' he confided to James. 'She has invited me to visit her again.'

James noticed the sparkle in his eyes. 'Then I'm glad that you have found a common bond, although, if I may say so, surprised. A lady of the aristocracy and a seafarer, indeed!'

Later, as James was getting ready to leave, Lady Burlington approached him, assuming a confidential manner. 'Thank you, James, for introducing Francis to me. I find him a most agreeable gentleman. A man of the world, indeed. So knowledgeable,' she said admiringly.

As she kissed him goodbye, James could not help but reflect on how happy a countenance she had.

17

No longer a king-in-waiting but as the appointed King George III, George took up residence in Buckingham House, together with both his wife and mother. He continued to reside in Kew Palace during the summer months but took on an active interest in the politics, often open to the criticism of parliamentarians. James read in the news-sheets that the Earl of Bath, an experienced politician, voiced his concern about the young king.

'George would have a very troublesome reign but that if the country had a little good fortune abroad, and obtained a good peace, and show that we are determined to pursue steadily right and popular measures at home and above all that the king appears to be resolute and steadfast, I think numbers may be persuaded to stick by the young king rather than old ministers.' Also that, 'The king's mind was more occupied with ending the war with France and restoring peace to his people. He strongly assured the French ambassador that peace was equally necessary for both kingdoms.'

James realised that the onerous duties of kingship was distancing George from him, but George insisted that James continued to visit him when he was in residence in Kew Palace. The occasions when he did often coincided with meeting Lord Wysop, who continued to show his animosity to James, being even more resentful of the king not heeding his advice to end his friendship with James, when in all other matters, George looked to Lord Wysop for guidance and was dependant on it and had let it be known that "anyone who speaks against Wysop speaks against me", making James very cautious in voicing any criticism of him. On the other hand, George's friendship and support of James was continually tested by Lord Wysop, who, to salve his own conscience, lost no opportunity to show James in an unfavourable light.

However, James's mother-in-law, Elisabeth, still had not got over Lord Wysop's unfaithfulness and that despite her denunciation of him, he had inveigled himself into the Dowager Princess Augusta's favours or, more likely, she thought, her heart. She felt consumed by jealousy and, like a cancer, her jealousy had grown within her. Her public denunciation of him had not provoked him into answering the accusation as she had expected, and his continued silence had left her unsatisfied and outraged. She vowed to continue to get her revenge and to republish her denunciation of Lord Wysop in the *London Daily Advertiser* by exposing his failure to rebut her accusation. The paper was only too ready to concede to her request on the proviso that she updated the readers on her further thoughts and added to her denunciation. They knew a good story when they had one and were happy to exploit it. Elisabeth was well aware of their motives, of course, but as they coincided with her own wishes to gain maximum exposure of her denunciation of the lord she happily agreed. The paper reignited it as a love story gone wrong between a titled personage and a commoner, and repeated its original story, "**Actress Accuses Lord of Deceit**" with a follow-up under the heading "**Failure of Lord to Answer Accusation**", calling on Lord Wysop to reply to the accusation or risk public censure and assumption of guilt by his continued silence.

Lord Wysop was outraged when he read it and knew he was being looked upon as an object of ridicule by friends and foe alike. Not only was he a member of the nobility but he had his position in the House and in society to lose as well as his friendship with Princess Augusta, whose name and reputation was now publicly associated with his and even satirised and ridiculed in journals. He decided after much deliberation that he that had no other choice but to reply and to deny the accusation, if only in the interests of the princess.

The London paper was only too ready to oblige to run the story and agreed with the lord to publish his reply, albeit with some embellishment.

"**Lord Wysop Rebuffs Actress's Claim**"

Note: In fairness to both parties of a dispute, this paper upholds its tradition to give each side the opportunity and right of reply, and as we published **Miss Elisabeth Butler's** '**Accusation of Deceit**', we are therefore publishing the accused **Lord Wysop's** reply at his request. Please note that we do not hold any legal responsibility for the claims expressed by either party.

"**Actress Accuses Lord of Deceit**"

Notice has been taken of a repeated **Accusation** by the former **Actress**, **Miss Elisabeth Butler**, that I **deceived** her while in a '**loving relationship**' with her. I hereby deny her claim that I am now, or ever have been, in any relationship with her. Furthermore, I will instigate all necessary **legal proceedings** against anyone repeating this **False and Malicious Allegation** by word or by mouth.
Lord Samuel Wysop

Elisabeth's rage was intensified when she read the reply and readily accepted the paper's offer to publish her response as follows:

"**Actress Accuses Lord of Deceit**"

As a **grieving mother** who accepted the **offered**

hand of condolence and **friendship of Lord Wysop** and later entered into a **loving relationship** with him, it further grieves me that he publishes a **denial** of our loving relationship which was **consummated** early in our relationship. His **denial** is not one that I would expect of a gentleman, let alone a **Lord of the Realm**, and therefore I **challenge him to fulfil his threat** and to instigate his **legal proceedings** against me and bring **my accusation** to a **court of justice**, where I have no doubt that such a court **will rule in my favour**.
Signed: **Miss Elisabeth Butler**.

Lord Wysop almost suffered an apoplexy when he read the report. His whole reputation was being held up to public ridicule by this woman and by countering her accusation he had brought himself into the glare of public censure. He considered that any further statement or rebuttal he made would only add more fuel to the fire. He had been wrong to reply to her accusation in the first instance. It was not the public censure which grieved him more but that of his relationship with the king and the king's mother, Princess Augusta. How, he asked himself, was he to face up to them and defend his reputation in the House and in society?

18

James was surprised when an invitation arrived announcing the marriage of Lady Dorothy Burlington, widow, to Francis Boniface, widower, at St Nicholas, Chiswick, together with a request from Francis asking James to be his best man at the wedding. James was delighted at the news and that the two good friends of his had found love for each other, and he readily accepted the honour.

James felt a glow of pride when he witnessed the marriage ceremony and remembered that when he had introduced them to each other he had never expected this outcome. At the reception, held at Chiswick House, he made his best man's speech to the assembled guests, and Francis followed with his speech of thanks to James for first introducing him to Dorothy, known only as Lady Burlington by many of the guests. He recalled how he first met James on board the good ship *Annabelle*, named after the captain's daughter and who later became his first wife.

Lady Burlington followed with her thanks to all the guests and special thanks to James for introducing her to Francis and humorously expressing the hope that she would meet the standards set by both of the "Annabelle"s, wife and ship.

Among the many guests was James's mother-in-law, Elisabeth, who, without commenting on the occasion, lost no time in taking his arm and relating her censure of Lord Wysop.

James listened patiently before answering. 'I am no friend of Lord Wysop, indeed, far from it, but if what you say is true and he has had a change of heart then, I agree, he should have told you so. It was between yourselves and I don't think you did yourself any favours by making it public.'

'But he is casting me aside and I think he owes me a public apology as well as recompense for his behaviour. We were to be married. I will take up his challenge and repeat my accusation. Then he will have to carry out his threat of legal action or he will never be able to hold his head up in public again,' said Elisabeth, showing her anger.

'Then I am truly sorry for you, although I think you might have regrets. He will always act in his own interests and I think he has bigger fish to fry, if I am honest,' replied James.

'Then he will have to answer to his bigger fish, if you mean Princess Augusta, and how do you think she will react to his behaviour? He will not be doing himself any favours with her, will he? She has her own reputation to think about, as well as her status as the king's mother,' argued Elisabeth.

'I do grant you that you will be stirring up a hornet's nest, but is that what you want? Revenge? You must remember that he is advisor to the king, as well, and King George will not take kindly to his mother being dragged into your public accusation. Besides, George thinks very highly of Lord Wysop. He's known him since boyhood and he's got the king's interests at heart,' said James.

Elisabeth looked determined. 'So be it, but I will repeat my accusation,' she said vehemently, 'and if he takes legal action, I will fight it.'

James realised that there was no gainsaying his mother-in-law and moved on to engage with other guests when he found himself stopping to talk with one of the bridesmaids. He soon realised that she knew more about him than he did of her. The thought increased his interest, and from questioning her he discovered a strong liking for her and a stirring within himself that he had not felt since first meeting Hannah.

She introduced herself as Daphne Boyle and said that she was related to the late Richard Boyle, Lord Burlington, which induced an even greater interest in her by James as he recalled the friendliness and help he had received from him.

'Ah, he was a true friend and patron and gave me a lot of support in my music, as did Lady Burlington.'

'Yes, Dorothy is my aunt,' she explained. 'I suppose now that she will drop her title and be known as Mrs Boniface. It's a lovely name to have, isn't it?'

'Boniface? Yes. If you can live up to it, which I think your aunt certainly does,' replied James with a laugh. 'But she will still be Lady Burlington to me. I have a lot of respect for her, you know.'

'We all have, in the family, but it's nice to know that others have, too. She is very caring,' Daphne said.

As their conversation continued, and with Daphne showing an encouraging interest, James was induced into recalling his past and his aspirations to her, feeling an ease and familiarity which surprised himself.

'So glad that you two have met each other. I was going to introduce you,' said Lady Burlington, approaching them.

'We were just discussing whether you will be known by your married name or your title,' said Daphne.

'Oh, Mrs Boniface, I hope,' she replied. 'But I expect that officially I will keep my title. I would still like to be remembered by society as Lady Burlington, if only in memory of Richard, whom I still hold dear.'

'That is an advantage that your title gives you,' said Daphne. 'A choice of names? Not something we all have.'

'Well, it's not something I think a lot about. I'm still Dorothy to my friends. I'm not sure what advantage a title gives, but society seems to demand it. People will have to get used to Mrs Boniface now, for that is who I am and I want the world to know.'

Francis approached with a radiant smile on his face. 'Did I hear our name mentioned?' he asked of Dorothy.

'Yes, and I am very happy to answer to it, Francis, my dear,' she said, turning to James and Daphne. 'I do apologise. You were engaged in a conversation before I interrupted, so we will leave you both to get on with it.'

'Who would have thought it?' questioned Daphne of James after Lady Burlington's departure. 'My aunt finding love with a common sailor? I always thought she was the epitome of convention.'

'She has never been anything other than gracious to me. Never without encouragement and help,' said James. 'As was your uncle, Lord Burlington.'

'Oh, yes, Uncle Richard. He was dedicated to music and even had Handel staying with him at Burlington House for months. Handel wrote and dedicated some of his operas to him while he was there, you know.'

James felt the affection he had for Daphne increase as he listened to her. He had missed the warm, satisfying feeling of love since the death of Hannah and now felt the glimmerings of love again.

'Yes, he gave me so much encouragement and opened his house for my concerts. I am, indeed, very indebted to him and to Lady Dorothy. I hope that she finds happiness again with Francis. I think she will.'

'You must miss your wife,' she said sympathetically.

'Yes, but I hold her memory dear and that will never go,' replied James. 'She died after giving birth to our child, unfortunately.'

'You have a child?' Daphne asked in surprise.

'Yes, I named him Henry, after the sea captain, Henry Cudlip, who gave me my name and brought me here from Jamaica. I have a nursemaid to look after him.'

'Oh, I would love to see him. How old is he now?'

Before James could reply, Elisabeth sidled up to them, smiling engagingly. 'Do introduce me to the young lady, James.'

James sighed to himself. Elisabeth was obviously in the mood to relate her problems to whoever would listen and he felt that there was going to be an outpouring of them now she had a new listener.

'Oh, I'm sorry. This is my mother-in-law, Elisabeth Butler,' said James.

'Pleased to meet you, my dear. You remind me of my dear late daughter, Hannah, James's wife,' replied Elisabeth. 'But you must be younger than she would have been now?'

'I'm nineteen,' Daphne said obligingly. 'Daphne Boyle. Very pleased to meet, madam.'

'Boyle? Related to the Burlingtons then, are you?'

'Yes, the dear Lord Burlington was my uncle.'

'Oh, I knew Lord Burlington, Richard, very well indeed. Very well,' said Elisabeth with a snide insinuation. 'A lovely, kind gentleman. There are so few of them nowadays.'

'I'm sorry if you don't meet many,' sympathised Daphne.

Elisabeth appraised the response. She was not happy or used to being the object of sympathy, and certainly not from another woman and one younger than herself.

'I have high standards. I suppose that is the reason,' Elisabeth countered. 'In fact, I am in a legal dispute with a lord at the moment, would you know it? I have my reputation to uphold. A matter of broken promises, but it's gone beyond that now.'

'Oh, who is that, may I ask?' questioned Daphne.

'Lord Wysop, my dear. We were to be married.'

'I'm sorry,' said Daphne.

'You do not need to be sorry for me, my dear. Sorry for him, yes. He has a lot to lose,' Elisabeth replied vehemently. 'He will know when I start my legal proceedings.'

James felt that Elisabeth was about to relate her recriminations against Lord Wysop again and diverted the conversation back to Lord Burlington, prompting Elisabeth to move away and seek another listener.

James gave Daphne a quizzical look before resuming his conversation with her. 'Did you know that Lord Burlington was godfather to the king and his sister, Princess Augusta?' he asked her. 'I was tutor to them both in their childhood and we still correspond. I knew her as Gusta in those days. She married the prince of Brunswick against her mother's wishes, but it has turned out to be a very happy marriage. In fact, I had a letter from her only yesterday telling me that she had given birth to her first child, a daughter, and was so very happy. She wrote that no two people could live better than they do and that she would go through fire and water for her husband. Amazing!' James exclaimed.

'It sounds like a marriage made in heaven,' replied Daphne.

'Yes, I'm so happy for her,' said James after reflection. 'There is nothing to compare to a happy marriage, I'm sure.'

James lapsed into silence as he reflected on his past marriage and wondered how he could possibly hope to recapture it. He looked earnestly at Daphne. How could he, a black man and widower with a child, expect her, a young woman of the aristocracy, to return his affection?

'Love conquers all, don't they say?' said Daphne coquettishly.

James's heart beat faster at the remark. That was the answer he wanted to hear. 'How true. I'm sure it goes a long way. Would you like to visit me at home to see Henry?'

'Oh, yes. My sister, Edith, can accompany me.'

'You would both be very welcome. I'll look forward to it.'

When Daphne did visit, her sister, who looked older and assumed the role of chaperon, sat between them and seldom took her eyes off James, looking curiously at him but saying little. James felt her presence intimidating, even more so by her curiosity and questioning of his background which, as he briefly related it to her, seemed to give her increasing cause for concern.

'And you have a child?' asked Edith. The question was asked more as an admission of guilt than an enquiry.

'Yes, Henry, he's two now,' replied James, and, calling to his housemaid, asked her to bring Henry to him.

As they waited, the atmosphere in the room chilled, with Daphne's sister sitting bolt upright in silence with a censorious look on her face.

'Oh, he's lovely,' Daphne cried out as the child was brought into the room.

She bent down to lift the child up, kissed him and held him close. Henry showed no resistance but relaxed into her arms and smiled up to her as she kissed him again and again.

Her spinster sister frowned. 'Don't get so carried away, Daphne.'

James looked on and felt reassured by the child's ready acceptance of Daphne. It was all he could have wished for.

The next day, James received a letter from Daphne thanking him for his friendship but saying that it was more than friendship she felt for him and she knew now that she loved him. James was overjoyed and immediately wrote back to say her love was reciprocated and proposed marriage. When Daphne confided her love to her sister, Edith informed their mother and father who, when they learnt of James's antecedents, foresaw impending disaster and dishonour for their daughter.

Amid tears, the distraught Daphne defended her love, but the more that was revealed of James to them – that he was coloured, a widower and a father – the greater their determination to stop the marriage. Despite pleading from their daughter, they refused their consent. Daphne suggested to James that she would run away with him to marry, but James argued against it, with Daphne being under the age of twenty-one and citing the likelihood of her parents bringing a charge of kidnapping against him, and that it would understandably cause even more resentment against him by her parents. Finally, after more and more pleading from their daughter, and on learning that James was a talented musician and enjoyed the friendship of no less a person than the king himself, they quickly relented and said that they would defer their decision until after they had met him.

James was delighted to accept the invitation and, on his arrival with his boy, proudly holding his hand, his refined appearance and manner immediately led them to question their previously biased concerns. When introductions had been made and their enquires reassuringly answered, any animosity Daphne's parents held were spirited away and, to the delight of Daphne and James, they gave their wholehearted consent to the marriage.

19

Elisabeth's wrath showed no sign of abating while she waited for Lord Wysop to accept the *London Daily Advertiser*'s published offer and bring legal proceedings against her. With none forthcoming from Lord Wysop, she accepted the newspaper's invitation to keep the topical story running and repeat her accusation and thereby possibly force his hand. The newspaper knew their readers' interest in the story was growing and repeated her accusation.

> "**Actress Accuses Lord of Deceit**"
>
> With the expressed endorsement of the **actress Miss Elisabeth Butler**, and of many of our **women readers**, this newspaper is proud to continue to **expose men** of whatever rank or none, who take advantage of the emotions of the **weaker sex** and to this end **we publish** even if we are **damned** by them! **Editor**
>
> **Lord Wysop** has failed to fulfil his **threat** to instigate **legal proceedings** against me which **I challenged him** to do. **His silence speaks volumes.** Does he realise that he would lose out to the truth? Is he afraid that his **duplicity** would be **publicly exposed** in a **Court of Justice**? I act on behalf

of all women who have succumbed to the charms of men only to find that they have succumbed to charlatans or imposters. I herewith repeat my **accusation against Lord Wysop** for a breach of promise and will instigate legal proceedings against him and pursue him in the **Court of Justice**.

Signed: **Miss Elisabeth Butler**.

Elisabeth read her challenge printed in the newspaper and felt a glow of satisfaction that she was leading a crusade for all women deceived by men's promises, but, as Lord Wysop maintained his silence and did not oblige, the satisfied feeling was slowly tempered by the likely costs that a legal challenge would accrue, and without an engagement ring or evidence of a promise, the likelihood of her challenge succeeding would be slim indeed. Lacking any admission or further response from Lord Wysop, Elisabeth's determination for revenge faltered but continued to fester in her mind.

With both revenge and jealousy clamouring for satisfaction and a continued silence from her alleged seducer, Elisabeth wrote a letter to the editor of the *London Daily Advertiser*, saying that, following her published accusation, she had a story to tell which, if the paper dare print it, would expose the hypocrisy of the ruling elite. The editor, ever eager to publish scandal or revelation of misdeeds, invited her for interview, but on hearing her accusation against Lord Wysop repeated, showed little inclination to publish it again. However, when Elisabeth mentioned Lord Wysop's association with the Dowager Princess of Wales, he detected a good story and, with Elisabeth's enhanced contribution, put the story to print.

Eager as ever to fully expose the injustice, she claimed, Elisabeth also contacted John Wilkes, writer and proprietor of the popular newspaper *The North Briton* and no lover of the monarch to also publish her story, to which he was happy to oblige, together with a cartoon showing Lord Wysop with his trousers down and with an extended tongue licking the arse of the Dowager Princess of Wales and a caption reading, "Better than a hogshead of cider".

When Lord Wysop saw the cartoon, he nearly had an apoplexy and considered legal action against the newspaper but decided instead to maintain his stance of silence and not to give the accusation further legs by contesting it and possibly exposing himself to further public ridicule.

Elisabeth felt vindicated by the public exposure of her former suitor and was given the original cartoon by the newspaper, which she had framed and proudly hung it in her parlour, showing it off to whoever came to visit her. (But after a while she found the constant reminder of Lord Wysop it gave her to be an irritant and finally put it out of her sight and out of her mind.)

From his knowledge of the law, Lord Wysop also had unsurprisingly already come to the same conclusion as Elisabeth and that in the unlikely event that she brought proceedings against him for a breach of promise to marry, it would fail on lack of evidence and could only be decided by his word against hers. The views of an actress against that of a peer of the realm would more than likely be derided, he surmised. He smiled to himself as he relished the thought of the privileges that his peerage, with its prestige, bestowed on him.

He was far too preoccupied in the House of Lords with parliamentary work and gathering support for the Government over the American war for independence and the continuing war with France to maintain a personal war against Elisabeth's accusations. He had moved a Parliamentary Bill to pay for the wars by the imposition of a tax on cider of four shillings per hogshead. A new tax, for which Lord Wysop, unsurprisingly, was blamed for by the press and which damaged popular support for the Government, with protestors taking to the streets and riots breaking out, particularly in the West Country, where most of the cider was made and which had many elected MPs.

The growing demand from America for independence would

not only mean the end of British government over the colony but also the end of the rule of monarchy over it, the thought of which greatly antagonised the king as ruler over the Dominions as well as Great Britain. Was he to go down in history as the king who lost the Americas? The thought greatly disturbed him and diminished his opinion of Lord Wysop as his trusted advisor. The one thing the king wanted above all others was to be popular with his people, but the tide of popular opinion against his government over the cider tax reverberated on him.

Lord Wysop, however preoccupied as he was with state affairs, was anxious to maintain his relationship with the king as well as his intimacy with the king's mother, Princess Augusta. Nevertheless, despite his responsibilities, his thoughts were constantly disturbed by the knowledge that James had of him, but more so, of James's close friendship and familiarity with the king.

James had accepted an offer from Dr Lucas to speak again at a meeting against slavery and injustice, which ended in a brawl and fisticuffs fight. On this occasion it was printed and unfavourably reported on in news-sheets and portrayed as being another attack against the established order and as an incitement to public discord. Much to his great surprise and consternation, police came to James's home and served him with an immediate arrest warrant for suspicion of seditious libel, took him to prison and locked him in a cell to await trial the next day. After an anxious and sleepless night in prison, he was brought before the bench and charged for seditious libel.

James felt nervous as he stood in the dock waiting for the judge to enter the court. He looked up to the public benches and saw his mother-in-law, Elisabeth, sitting alone, resplendent in white, Daphne smiling nervously at him, sitting with her sister, Edith, and next to her, Dr Lucas and his wife, Susie, who waved to him and blew a kiss. John Wilkes, of *The North Briton*, sat engrossed in reading his own newspaper and looking stern, as if he had just spotted a mistake.

James pleaded not guilty, and on questioning from the judge, he answered that as a free man he was entitled by the law of the land to speak against the established order. The judge looked down on him benignly and said that he accepted his plea of not guilty, but in his summing-up, he gave a warning to James that he had come close to inciting civil unrest and warned him of the possible consequences if he had. James breathed a sigh of relief and stepped down to freedom again and into the arms of Daphne amid the congratulations of his friends and his mother-in-law, Elisabeth. On the next day, *The North Briton* blazoned the trial on its front page and held James up as a man of the empire and defender of ancient English liberties.

Lord Wysop only too readily seized on the judge's warning of James inciting civil unrest as evidence to denigrate James to King George at their next meeting and claimed it showed James's disloyalty to king and country. George tacitly accepted his argument, but in defence of James argued that James's views could only be expected, given his background of being of colour and born of a slave and that, as a long-standing friend of James going back to his childhood, he was not going to take the criticism of the justice system as an attack on him personally, much to the chagrin of Lord Wysop.

20

It was whilst she was sitting in the court and witnessing the trial of her son-in-law that Elisabeth had second thoughts about her decision not to bring charges against Lord Wysop for breach of promise. His public ridicule was hardly compensation for her loss, and a cartoon, whilst amusing to the public, was neither vindication or sufficient recompense for her suffering, she reasoned. She had threatened legal proceedings against him but had failed to carry out her threat, despite his continued silence. Now, she thought, she had a duty to carry out her threat and engage a prosecutor or face further ridicule. The cost of legal action if she lost the case weighed on her mind but was offset by the possible compensation award she might receive if she won. She decided to put it to her son-in-law, James, for his opinion.

James was in a euphoric state of mind when Elisabeth met him. He was in true love for the second time in his life and he had enjoyed the acclamation of the press for standing up as a defender of English liberties. Never had he known the satisfaction he now felt, except that neither achievements added to his wealth, or his lack of it. His music engagements had been curtailed, particularly since Lady Burlington had accepted the more private nondescript name of Mrs Boniface and no longer hosted recitals, and with payment for his tutorials of the king's children still awaited. Like all acclaimed receivers of royal patronage, the patronage was considered payment enough, and promised financial payment took a long time to materialise if ever it came to be fulfilled.

It was, therefore, with unexpected relief to James when Daphne's father spoke to him of a considerable dowry he had set upon his daughter, and that he knew that love came first but that he could not imagine a better man than James receiving the dowry or to have a better son-in-law.

James's euphoric state of mind was quickly subdued when Elisabeth confronted him with her problems. 'James, I am going to carry out my threat to bring legal proceedings against Lord Wysop. He has never made any response to my accusation. Oh, I know he thinks I won't take any action, but I will prove him wrong. I know I have good grounds for recompense from him. Don't you agree?'

James gave the question some thought. He had hoped he had turned his back on legal proceedings, having spent so many anxious hours of late in a courtroom. 'I think you may have. He has never denied your accusation, has he?'

'No, he hasn't. That would be in my favour, wouldn't it?'

'I would think so, but one can never be sure of the outcome of legal action. You would have to consider your situation and the cost to you if you lost.'

'I don't believe I would lose it, James.'

'But you have no hard evidence. It's only your word against his, surely? The word of a man of rank and title would carry more weight than yours would. You would be seen as a woman scorned and embittered.'

'And what would I be if I didn't carry out my threat? A false and weak woman! No, I will pursue him in court and engage an attorney.'

The resolution, previously only in her mind and now a stated commitment, emboldened Elisabeth in her determination for revenge, as she saw herself as leading for the rights of maligned and deserted women wounded by men's disloyalty and sought for an attorney.

Lord Wysop was surprised and enraged to subsequently receive notification from the attorney stating that an application had been made to the Ecclesiastical Court, on behalf of Elisabeth Butler, to bring a charge against him of breach of promise to marry. He had underestimated her and misjudged her determination to implement her threat. He was already burdened by his parliamentary work and gathering support for the Government over the American war and also feared of losing the approbation of the king if his own integrity became a matter of public debate.

His fears were justified when the cartoon by John Wilkes was brought to the notice of the king and his relationship with the king's mother, the Dowager Princess of Wales, was revealed to the king. Lord Wysop felt extreme anger and annoyance at the thought of the disrepute and public ridicule it would bring, not just to himself but also to the king and the royal family, and which would be attributed to him.

Furthermore, he suspected that the public backlash from his imposition of his cider tax was shared by the king who, no doubt, would think he had been ill-advised by him and would turn against him. He would be publicly humiliated by litigation being brought against him and the likelihood of him losing it. Finally, although somewhat reluctantly, he succumbed to instructing his attorney to consult with Elisabeth's attorney for a possible out-of-court settlement and thereby avoiding further public humiliation over a breach of promise and possible ostracism by other members in the House of Lords.

Elisabeth was elated and gratified when she received the news from her attorney, but, on reflection, felt that if she accepted, she would be letting Lord Wysop off too lightly, foregoing her denunciation of him in the glare and transparency of public censure and decided to consult with her son-in-law, James, for his thoughts.

James made it plain that he had not changed his opinion. 'If you pursued him in court, you may well lose your case, and where would that leave you? In the glare of public humiliation and a large legal bill to pay. You have no written evidence. No, accept his offer. Take advice from your attorney as to how much you can expect to settle for out of court. Lord Wysop must be financially well off and anxious for it to be settled.'

Elisabeth considered his proposal for a moment. 'No, I want the satisfaction of exposing him publicly. Our relationship goes back a long way and can be verified by many people whom I can call on. It was no secret and he cannot deny it.'

James realised that his mother-in-law was not to be diverted from the satisfaction of getting revenge and that not even money would compensate for being rejected. 'Well, then, you must go ahead with it, although what good you can get from it, I don't know. Judges can't force a man to carry out a promise to marry, can they? Anyway, would you want to be married to him now, after all this?'

His advice only made Elisabeth more determined than ever to pursue her claim in court, if only for the satisfaction of exposing the injustice of unfulfilled promises made to women by men. On consulting her attorney, he confirmed James's view and advised her that the evidence for a breach of promise, without written evidence, was too weak to succeed and advised her against taking it to court, to accept the lord's offer and settle out of court.

At first, Elisabeth felt humiliated and distraught at his advice, but, on reflection, it only made her more determined than ever to sue for breach of promise whilst continuing her public denunciation of Lord Wysop. When her case eventually came to court, Elisabeth was furious when the judge court summarily dismissed her claim on lack of evidence but was even more so when she learnt that Lord Wysop had consequently withdrawn his offer for settlement out of court. Now, all that was left for her was to continue her personal vendetta and vilification of him, which, to her dismay, she eventually found soon lost its news value through her repetition.

21

Lord Wysop's entreaties to the king to disassociate himself from James fell on deaf ears with his own influence on George greatly diminished. King George retained an affection for James going back to his childhood and which continued to be shared by his own growing number of children, the older of whom received musical instruction from James. On hearing from his children that James was going to get married again, the king invited James to visit and to introduce his fiancée to Court.

When James arrived at Court, the king surprised him by saying that he would be awarding him the Order of the Garter for his services to king and country. James was overwhelmed with gratitude but had to contain his excitement until the honour was officially announced. He confided the news to Daphne, who confided it to her parents and her sister and to his mother-in-law, Elisabeth, who confided it to everyone she knew.

When the day for the investiture ceremony arrived, James, accompanied by Daphne and his son, Henry, went to Windsor Castle to receive the honour from the king, who expressed his appreciation for everything that James had done for him and his children, before formally presenting him with the Garter Star medal and sash of the Order. Two senior knights placed the garter around James's left leg and fastened the riband around his body, and together they joined the other knights in their procession to St George's Chapel.

As a member of the Order, he now took on the title of Knight Companion, thereby endorsing its motto, "*Honi soit qui mal y pense*" ("Shame on him who thinks evil of it") and the official title of honour, "Sir". Now, as Sir James Cudlip, Knight Companion of the Order of the Garter and, in addition, his entitlement to sit in the House of Lords, James accepted his new responsibilities with equanimity but, underneath, with a feeling of unreality when he recalled his origins and childhood. The unpredictability of his achievements from being born a slave to his present status was always at the back of his mind. None more so now that he was to take his seat in the House on an equal par with his long-time adversary and would-be subjugator, Lord Wysop.

On James being introduced to the House, Lord Wysop could not hide his distain and openly spoke of the House of Lords damaging its authority to govern by admitting colonial ex-slaves into its chambers. James welcomed the opportunity it gave him to reply and spoke of his own experience of the slave trade, freedom and democracy, which was enthusiastically received in the House with cheers and back-slapping.

Lord Wysop's own authority was already greatly diminished in the House and in the country, not only because of his unpopularity over his introduction of the cider tax and the damaging lampooning of him in the popular broadsheets, particularly of his relationship with the dowager princess, but also because of Elisabeth's public humiliation and exposure of him, which made him even more so a figure of ridicule. His relationship with the king would be tested and, he feared, he would possibly be ostracised, not only by the king but also by the king's mother, the dowager princess, putting an end to their intimacy.

Lord Wysop's fears were born out when he did find himself being ostracised in the House and by his contemporaries, which hurt him deeply. He regrettably left the front bench and, after fading into the obscurity of the back benches, he eventually withdrew from politics altogether to spend more time unchallenged in his fiefdom in the wilds of Scotland.

Daphne happily agreed to James's suggestion for their wedding to be held in his parish church of St Nicholas, where their banns were duly registered, and fore-called over the preceding three weeks. Daphne's sister, Edith, was the bridesmaid; and Henry, James's son, and Ben, who owed his freedom to James, were the ushers. Once again, James walked up the aisle and made his vows, but on making the vow of "until death do us part", he was overcome by emotion as he recalled making the same vow to Hannah and briefly halted the ceremony.

Dorothy put Chiswick House at his disposal for the following reception, and guests included Elisabeth and her daughter, Caroline, Dr Thomas Lucas and his wife, Susie, William Hogarth and his wife, Jane, Felicity and her husband George, as well as Dorothy and her husband Francis. Surprise congratulatory greetings were read out from King George and his family to the clapping of the guests.

Afterword

King George III (b1738–d1820). Reigned from 1760 to 1820.

Prince Frederick (b1763–d1827). Heir presumptive king from 1820 and king to 1827.

King George IV (b1762–d1830). Reigned from 1820 to 1830.